Dad piped up, 'The thing is, Marcus, you're special.'

'Oh, I'm the best.' I grinned. 'And I'm so glad you've realized it – at long last.'

'But a few extra things are going to happen to you, which your friends won't experience,' he continued.

'Like what?' I asked cautiously.

'Well, you will smell quite horrid,' said Mum.

I sniffed my armpits. 'Are you saying I stink?' I asked.

'No, no,' said Mum, 'but you will for a little while, or rather your breath will. And there's nothing you can do to take away the smell.'

'And soon,' said Dad, 'a white fang will appear in your mouth.'

I gaped at him. 'Dad, what on earth are you talking about?'

www.randomhousechildrens.co.uk

www.petejohnsonauthor.com

How many Pete Johnson books have you read?

Funny stories

THE BAD SPY'S GUIDE
*Shortlisted for the 2007 Blue Peter Book Award
Book I Couldn't Put Down category*
'This book grabs you from the first page (5 stars)' *Sunday Express*

HELP! I'M A CLASSROOM GAMBLER
Winner of the 2007 Leicester Our Best Book Award
'A real romp of a read that will leave readers ravenous for more' *Achuka*

HOW TO GET FAMOUS
Winner of the Sheffield Community Libraries Prize

HOW TO TRAIN YOUR PARENTS
'Makes you laugh out loud' *Sunday Times*

RESCUING DAD
'Most buoyant, funny and optimistic' *Carousel*

THE TV TIME TRAVELLERS
'Another great humorous book from critically acclaimed Pete Johnson'
Literacy Times

TRUST ME, I'M A TROUBLEMAKER
*Winner of the 2006 Calderdale Children's Book of the Year
(Upper Primary)*

Thrillers

AVENGER
*Winner of the 2006 Sheffield Children's Book Award,
Children's Books, shorter novel
Winner of the 2005 West Sussex Children's Book Award*
'Brilliant' *Sunday Express*

THE CREEPER
'Explores the subtle power of the imagination' *Books for Keeps*

THE FRIGHTENERS
'Prepare to be thoroughly spooked' *Daily Mail*

THE GHOST DOG
Winner of the 1997 Young Telegraph / Fully Booked Award
'Incredibly enjoyable' *Books for Keeps*

TRAITOR
'Fast-paced and energetic' *The Bookseller*

PHANTOM FEAR
Includes:
MY FRIEND'S A WEREWOLF and THE PHANTOM THIEF

EYES OF THE ALIEN
'Very readable with a skilful plot' *Observer*

PETE JOHNSON

THE VAMPIRE BLOG

CORGI BOOKS

THE VAMPIRE BLOG
A CORGI YEARLING BOOK 978 0 440 86935 1

Published in Great Britain by Corgi Yearling,
an imprint of Random House Children's Publishers UK
A Random House Group Company

This edition published 2010

11

Set in 12.5/16pt Century Schoolbook by
Falcon Oast Graphic Art Ltd.

Corgi Yearling Books are published by
Random House Children's Publishers UK,
61–63 Uxbridge Road, London W5 5SA

www.**randomhousechildrens**.co.uk
www.**randomhouse**.co.uk

Addresses for companies within The Random House Group Limited
can be found at: www.randomhouse.co.uk/offices.htm

THE RANDOM HOUSE GROUP Limited Reg. No. 954009

A CIP catalogue record for this book is available from
the British Library.

Penguin Random House is committed to a sustainable future for
our business, our readers and our planet. This book is made from
Forest Stewardship Council® certified paper.

MIX
Paper from
responsible sources
FSC® C018179

Printed and bound in Great Britain by Clays Ltd, Elcograf S.p.A.

To Bill – who knows a lot about vampires!

CHAPTER ONE

Sunday 30 September
7.15 p.m.

Three things you never want to hear your parents say:

'Let's talk about the facts of life.'

'We're going to start dancing now.'

'Soon, a white fang will appear in your mouth.'

My parents have just told me that last one. Then they went on to tell me ... well, you just wait.

Today is my thirteenth birthday. And for the first time in the history of the world, my parents bought me a present I actually wanted: an iPod Touch. It's got to be my

Christmas present as well. But I don't care. It's brilliant. And it's no bigger than a mobile phone so it can go anywhere with me. Now I can play video games or go on the internet or blog whenever I want.

And I imagined myself keeping such a sensational blog that just about everyone would be going mad to read it. Well, my blog's going to be sensational all right, but no one can ever see it. What I'm about to tell you, blog, is for your eyes only – and must remain hidden behind a secret password for ever.

Strange how your life changes when you're least expecting it. I was just innocently munching my tea tonight when Mum and Dad suddenly stormed in. Mum switched off the telly and she and Dad sat down at the table with me.

'We want to talk to you, Marcus,' said Dad.

This didn't surprise me. Mum and Dad are always giving me long, boring lectures which really annoy me. That's what I go to school for.

'We thought,' said Dad, 'this would be a good moment to tell you' – he looked at Mum, who nodded slightly – 'about some of the wonderful changes that will soon be taking place in your body.'

'Getting tons of acne and my voice going all wobbly, you mean,' I said.

'There are other changes too,' said Mum softly.

Oh no, here it comes, I thought, the facts of life talk. My toes were curling up with embarrassment already. 'Not while I'm eating, Mum, please. You'll put me right off,' I said. 'And we've done it in biology anyway, so I know all the gory details.' Then I smiled, looked hopefully at the door and said, 'Hey, Mum and Dad, it's been great hanging out with you both and don't be strangers now. Bye.'

But neither of them budged. Instead, they glanced quickly at each other again. Then Dad piped up, 'The thing is, Marcus, you're special.'

'Oh, I'm the best.' I grinned. 'And I'm so glad you've realized it – at long last.'

'But a few extra things are going to happen to you which your friends won't experience,' he continued.

'Like what?' I asked cautiously.

'Well, you will smell quite horrid,' said Mum.

I sniffed my armpits. 'Are you saying I stink?' I asked.

'No, no,' said Mum, 'but you will for a little while, or rather your breath will. And there's nothing you can do to take away the smell.'

'And soon,' said Dad, 'a white fang will appear in your mouth.'

I gaped at him. 'Dad, what on earth are you talking about?'

But he just rattled on. 'Now, the fang will only be there for a day. And it's nothing to worry about, quite natural for someone as special as you.'

Dad looked as if he was about to say a lot more, but then Mum cried, 'Well, I think that's enough information for our first little talk.' And she started to get up.

'Er, hold on,' I said. 'Just why is a fang coming my way? You'll be telling me next I'm turning into a vampire!'

I rolled around laughing after I'd said that. Well, the atmosphere had got very tense without me quite knowing why. So when in doubt, laugh. Laughing is what life should be all about. That's what I say anyway. Only I suddenly noticed that Mum and Dad weren't even smiling. And then I spotted little beads of sweat on Dad's forehead.

'Hey, you two are really freaking me out tonight, you know,' I cried. 'You've put me right off my food as well, and usually nothing in the world can do that . . . now, just tell me, what's going on?'

Dad said slowly, 'You're not a vampire.'

'No, well I never really thought I was,' I said. 'They don't even exist, do they?'

Dad didn't answer this, but then said, very slowly and carefully as if he was translating what he was saying from another language, 'Your mother and I are, we're proud to say, half-vampires, well, nearly half – probably about forty per cent vampire. But we call ourselves half-vampires and we believe you are one too.'

When you hear something as totally mind-boggling as that, you don't leap about and go mad (that comes later). No, you swallow very, very deeply and think: This is either a dream and pigs will fly through the window any second now. Or my parents have both

TOTALLY FLIPPED. Yes, that's what's happened. The stress of modern life has really got to them.

So, smiling in quite a kindly way at my loopy parents, I asked, 'Now, how long have you thought you're half-vampires? Let's start with you, Dad. Just sit back, relax and tell me all about it.'

'It's a bit of a shock when you first hear, isn't it?' said Dad.

'Yeah, it is really,' I said, 'especially when I don't believe a single word of it.'

'We shouldn't have told you like this,' said Mum. 'The manual said to break it to you in stages.'

'What manual?' I asked.

'Oh, just a little guide for people in this situation,' said Mum. 'And we so wanted to do it right.'

'So how many half-vampires are there?' I asked. 'Or is it just you two crazies – and now lucky old me, of course?'

'There are more of us than you might think,' said Dad.

He was saying everything so calmly, and he didn't seem as if he was cracking up.

'Look,' I burst out, 'correct me if I'm wrong, but don't vampires have big teeth and very dodgy habits? Oh yeah, and aren't they supposed to crumble into dust in the sun and live for five centuries? Hey, you're not going to tell me you're both two hundred and fifty years old now, are you?'

Mum and Dad actually relaxed a bit then, and smiled as Mum said, 'You mustn't believe all the stories. They're full of such wild exaggerations and we're only half-vampires, of course. But you know that neither your father nor I like the sun.'

And with a flash of shock I did remember how carefully Mum and Dad always wrapped up on sunny days. And we never went to hot places for our holidays either. In fact, Mum and Dad much preferred off-peak winter breaks. But I thought that was just because they were being a bit stingy with their money.

'We do like the odd trickle of blood,' went on Mum. 'It's remarkably refreshing actually. But only as a wonderful little treat now and again. And we do enjoy visiting graveyards at night; well, they're just so full of atmosphere.'

'But we're no older than you think,' continued Dad. 'Half-vampires enjoy very long, active lives though. In fact, your great-grandmother lived long enough to see you when you were a little baby.'

Then Mum produced this photo of a remarkably ugly baby (me) sitting on the lap of a tiny woman who looked like a very battered doll.

'I've seen this picture before,' I said.

'But we never told you how old your great-grandmother was when this was taken,' said Mum excitedly. 'She was a hundred and twenty-four.'

'And she only looks a hundred and twenty-three,' I said. 'Amazing. So she was a half-vampire as well?'

'A very proud one too,' said Dad. 'She said our very long lives made us like time-lords. And she was active to the very end. Now, look at your grandparents . . . they might be retired, but neither your mother's parents nor mine want to just sit at home. They're all off travelling right now, aren't they?'

'But there is one important rule for us half-vampires,' said Mum. 'We must keep our identity secret. For if ordinary people knew about us . . .'

'We'd make them very nervous,' said Dad. 'There are just so many wild tales about us, so it's best they don't know what we are.'

'And I'm definitely a half-vampire?' I said.

'Almost certainly,' said Mum, 'but we'll know for definite in the next day or two. That's when these changes we mentioned should start.'

'So if I have disgusting breath and grow a fang I'm one of you?' I said.

Dad nodded slowly. 'But remember, there's nothing to worry about, only . . .' He hesitated.

'Yes?' I prompted.

Dad leaned forward. 'The difficult part for you will be over the next few days, when the vampire side of your nature tries to come through.'

'Just let that happen,' said Mum. 'Don't block it in any way. That's very important.'

'Any more questions?' asked Dad.

'Yeah, can you and Mum turn into bats?'

Mum actually blushed and Dad coughed

shyly. 'We don't like to show off . . . We'll tell you about that another day.'

'I can't wait,' I said, suddenly jumping up.

'Where are you going?' asked Mum.

'Off to ring the hospital, as you've both gone completely nuts.'

'Oh, Marcus,' cried Mum.

'I'm sorry, but there's weird and then there's this. I don't believe a word of it. I'm going out now.'

'No—' began Mum.

But Dad cut in. 'That's all right, let him stretch his legs for a few minutes.'

And I just tore outside.

8.25 p.m.

I had to get out of there. I mean, here were my parents telling me all this universe-shattering stuff, but in such a calm, everyday way. That really freaked me out. I tell you, blog, something very creepy is going on in my house.

Unless – well, it could just be a huge practical joke, of course. But my parents aren't into stuff like that. Or maybe it's some kind of test? My parents love anything educational. But what's educational about saying they're half-vampires?

No, I've got to just hope my parents have gone insane. And if they haven't . . . WHAT IS GOING ON?

Answers in blood on a gravestone.

9.05 p.m.

Went off on my skateboard for a bit, and then called on Joel, my best mate.

His mum answered the door, glaring hard, as usual. 'Oh, hello,' I said cheerily, 'is Joel there?'

'He's in disgrace,' she snapped, 'so you can see him for just five minutes. He's in his bedroom – where he'll stay for the rest of the night.'

Upstairs, Joel told me about his latest crime.

'Well, it was my little brother's birthday today and it was so boring . . . until I organized the biggest jelly fight you've ever seen.' He grinned. 'But I haven't forgotten it's your birthday and I have for you . . . a world-class card.'

I opened up the envelope. 'Hey, you made it yourself.'

'I spent several seconds on it too – and look at the bold way I wrote: HAPPY BIRTHDAY, MARCUS. There's even a little picture of a cake.'

'You spoil me.'

'So did anything exciting occur on your birthday?' asked Joel.

Sitting here in Joel's room, all that seemed far away now. I was right back in the normal world again. I showed him my iPod Touch, then I asked, 'Joel, would you say my parents are weird?'

'Oh yeah, but then all parents are.'

'But are mine especially weird?'

'Yeah, probably, but in a good way. I mean, your mum is nothing like mine. She's so laid back for a start, and she just drifts about the house in a dream. Not hot on the old house-work either, is she?'

This was true. Our house was full of arty pictures and books, but it was sort of messy too. I knew Mum hated disturbing cobwebs. And she wasn't the least bit scared of spiders either – in fact she treated them like little pets.

I suddenly pictured Mum with her long,

dark hair and all those jingly earrings she always wore. Yes, you could sort of imagine her slinking about in a horror film. But not Dad: a smallish man with a wispy beard and with an eager, helpful smile on his face and a trace of a Brummie accent. But he does have a study full of gory tales – shelves and shelves of them, in fact. Still, that doesn't prove anything. After all, he runs a bookshop. So why shouldn't he collect horror books?

'You're looking very thoughtful,' said Joel, 'or have you just got wind?'

9.50 p.m.

When I got back, my parents were waiting at the door for me.

'Ah, here he is,' said Dad, all smiley.

'Yeah, it's me. Not that I'm quite sure who I am right now – or who you are, come to that.'

'We've got something to show you,' said Dad. And when we went and sat down in the kitchen he handed me a little silver box. 'Maybe you've seen that in my study,' he said.

And I had, far away on a high shelf. I'd even vaguely wondered what was inside it.

'You can open it up,' said Dad.

I did, and inside was one small white fang. 'And this is yours?' I said.

'That's right,' said Dad proudly.

And seeing it and the look on Dad's face suddenly made everything they'd said seem horribly real.

'So this dangles off your mouth for a day,' I said, 'and then it just slips off?'

'That's right,' said Dad. 'You usually find it on your pillow the next morning. You get a bit of money for it too, as it's a sign your transformation into a half-vampire is underway. And when you've changed over, a second fang will appear – a yellow one.'

I nodded, slowly taking all this in. 'And you had fangs too, Mum?'

'Yes I did,' she said, 'but unfortunately I lost my white one. I really regret that now. I'll make sure we keep both your fangs safe.' Then Mum asked, all anxiously, 'So how do you feel about it all now?

'Me?' I grinned. 'I think it's all *fangtastic*.'

I'm such a liar sometimes.

CHAPTER TWO

Monday 1 October
8.30 a.m.

Bit of a weird atmosphere at breakfast. So to cheer things up I burst out, 'I expect you two would rather pour blood on your cereals than milk.'

Mum and Dad both looked very shocked. 'We never speak of such matters in the day-time,' hissed Mum.

'Not another word until nightfall,' said Dad firmly. 'And then only when we're alone.'

9.05 a.m.

There's a girl in my class called Tallulah. You can't miss her. She's got jet-black hair and has already been sent to the headmaster twice for wearing black nail varnish. She's only been here a short while, and all the other girls hate her already.

Anyway, this morning she jumped to the front of our classroom and said, 'I've got an announcement to make. And it won't interest most of you because you've got no personality.' There were a few muttered protests at this, but she had everyone's attention all right. 'I live on the dark side,' she said. 'And if there's anyone here like me . . .'

'There's no one in the world like you,' I called out. 'Thank goodness.'

'I'm starting a new secret organization called M.I.S.,' she went on, 'which stands for Monsters in School. We'll meet in a secret place tomorrow night and tell really scary tales about werewolves and zombies and, of course, my total favourites: vampires.'

That gave me a bit of a jolt. You don't hear anything about vampires for ages – and suddenly they're mentioned everywhere.

'I should warn you though, we'll be telling very gory stories, so if you're easily frightened don't even think of applying.'

'It's not the monsters who frighten me,' I called out, 'it's you.'

I'd only meant it as a joke but Tallulah gave me the full death stare. 'I knew, Marcus Howlett, that you'd have to try and be silly,' she snapped. 'And you're just a total wimp anyway.'

'Hey, I resent that,' I said. 'One of my toes is quite brave.'

She sighed heavily. 'If you want to know more about M.I.S. just ask me. I may not accept you as a member though.' She was looking right at me now. 'Because I'm very choosy who I allow to be in my society.'

'In fact, you might not even choose yourself,' I said.

Tallulah gave me another glare and stormed to her seat as the teacher came in.

'That girl,' I said to Joel, 'has all the charm of a rattlesnake.'

11.15 a.m.

You won't believe this, blog, but Joel has decided he's going to join M.I.S.

'You'd volunteer to spend a whole evening stuck in some grim dive, with her talking on and on about monsters?' I queried.

'I probably won't go back,' Joel admitted, 'but I'd like to try this M.I.S. once – just for the experience.'

'Well, it'll be just you and her,' I said.

'Oh no, you're wrong there,' said Joel. 'Others have been joining too. But I think they're only going along to laugh at her.' He grinned. 'Which is exactly why I'm going too.'

10.15 p.m.

This evening my dad announced: 'Got a little surprise for you.'

'Not another one,' I said.

'Ah, this is a present,' said Mum.

'My own pet bat?' I suggested.

'Come into the sitting room,' said Dad eagerly, 'so you can see your gift properly.'

I sidled in after them and Dad said, 'This belonged to me.'

'So it's a second-hand present. Wow, thanks.'

'Be quiet, dear,' said Mum. 'This is a very important moment.'

'Sorry,' I murmured.

'I believe the time has arrived,' said Dad,

'to pass this gift on to you.' Then he handed me a cape. It was black, with red lining and a pointy collar. And inside were Dad's initials, which are the same as mine. It was very heavy and nicely made. But it wasn't for me. I knew that, even before I tried it on.

It was too big for me for a start. 'You'll soon grow into it,' said Dad eagerly. 'Now, take a look at yourself in the mirror.'

'So vampires can see themselves then?' I asked.

'Of course,' said Mum. 'You might find your reflection goes a little bit misty over the next few weeks though.'

'Something else to look forward to,' I muttered, 'alongside bad breath and fangs.'

And then I saw myself in the mirror. And I looked so stupid, I burst out laughing. I laughed away until I noticed my parents weren't sharing the joke.

'Look,' said Dad, 'let me borrow it a moment.' He swiftly put the cape on, yet with such care too, as if he were handling something very precious.

'Hey, Dad, it suits you.'

And it did. Even though he's not very big,

the cape didn't take him over. It just made him look much more commanding somehow.

'I'll never forget the first time I put this on, just after my thirteenth birthday,' said Dad. 'And immediately it meant the world to me. And I just felt so proud to be part of—'

'The "We love blood" gang,' I quipped.

'Can we stop the silly comments for five seconds?' said Dad, his voice cracking with anger. 'Is that possible?'

'Yeah, all right, sorry,' I said.

'Because this means a great deal to your mother and me. We're proud of our heritage and . . .' Then Mum tapped his arm and Dad swallowed down what he was going to say next and just murmured, 'Try it again, it's your cape now, so come on, really wear it.'

I put the cape on again. And I did try to conjure up some enthusiasm for it. I even imagined I was a great magician. But the thing just didn't fit and flapped about very uneasily on me. In fact, I felt like a total fraud in it. 'Dad,' I said quietly, 'being a half-vampire could skip a generation, couldn't it?'

'It could,' murmured Dad quietly.

'Well, it has,' I said, even more quietly. 'So, Dad, have the cape back.'

'I've been looking forward to this moment for such a long time,' said Dad.

'I know, and I'm sorry – but if I'm not a half-vampire . . .'

Dad breathed heavily, and then said, 'I won't have the cape back. Hang it on your door and one day soon I know you will wear it with pride.'

I know I won't.

But I put the cape on my door. Only then I kept looking at it. And it's just as if my dad's left one of his suits in my room. That cape practically screams out, *I'm in the wrong place!* That's why in the end I bunged it in the wardrobe. I hung it up properly though.

Then I earwigged my parents, who were whispering away downstairs. Mum was saying, 'You frightened him tonight.'

Dad answered: 'The manual said we were to do this as soon as possible.'

'Yes, but you pushed him too hard,' replied Mum.

I can even feel a bit sorry for Dad, desperately wanting to pass the cape on to his son and all that. But he can't force me to change into something I'm not, can he?

Tuesday 2 October
6.30 a.m.

Awake already, checking for bad smells and fangs. All clear on both counts. I shan't be turning into a funky half-vampire today or any other day. I'm certain now it's skipped a generation. And I'm one hundred per cent human.

9.15 p.m.
Strange atmosphere at home tonight, very tense and yet eerily calm. Feels as if my parents are just waiting for something to happen. Only it never will.

9.45 p.m.
Joel just rang, fresh from the first-ever introductory M.I.S. meeting. 'Oooh, I wouldn't have missed it for anything. First of all, we met up with Tallulah.'

'Who are we?'

'Oh right, there were seven of us, all lads

from our class and her, and she took us into the woods.'

'Oooh-er.' I laughed.

'A secret place that I can't even tell you about. Well, I might in a minute. But anyway, she led us all in, and you know how the head-master looks when he's giving us a right telling-off in assembly, well that's exactly how Tallulah looked. She was dead stern.'

'I don't know how you kept a straight face,' I said.

'Oh, there's more,' said Joel. 'We all sat round in this secret place and she'd provided some food for us, which I thought was a thoughtful gesture. Next she told us a long, grisly tale which would have scared you, Marcus. Then she told us M.I.S. members must be ready at all times to shake up boring, everyday life – just as monsters do. So she's going to set us our first challenge soon. And our motto is just two words: *Monsters rule*. That's why if we want to come again we've got to wear a mask. No one will be admitted if they're not disguised as a monster. Then we left our secret meeting place.'

'Which was where?' I asked.

'Now, don't be offended, but I'm not going to tell you, because I did swear to keep the meeting place secret from everyone.'

'But you'll never go back again,' I said.

'Well, here's the funny thing, I think I will, as I've got a werewolf mask I haven't worn since Halloween about three years ago.'

'It probably won't even fit you now,' I said.

'But it's the thought that counts,' said Joel. 'And yeah, I'll go back just one more time as . . . well, just as I was leaving, Tallulah said that she was very surprised to see me there tonight – but actually she thinks I might have some monster potential.' Joel started to laugh again. 'I think that's the nicest thing anyone has ever said to me.'

Wednesday 3 October
7.05 a.m.

Terrible news!

I woke up to discover a horrible smell in my bedroom. Really foul, like rotting seaweed and the stinkiest fart you've ever smelled all mixed up together. It was totally disgusting.

Then I realized where the smell was coming from – me; or my mouth, to be more precise. I stank.

I sped off to the bathroom and started wildly brushing my teeth. But I just couldn't take away that stink from my mouth.

And then I noticed the bathroom door slowly opening. Mum was standing there, looking so triumphant.

'It's started, hasn't it?' she cried excitedly.

Chapter Three

Wednesday 3 October
8.45 a.m.

I'm still in bed. Mum said I can't possibly go to school today – and she's right. I'm a walking stink bomb. And if I so much as breathed on someone their nose would explode with shock.

'What exactly is that smell?' I asked Mum.

'It's perfectly normal and natural,' she replied Mum, looking ever so cheerful. 'Just a sign that the human part of you is resisting the intrusion of your brand-new vampire side. But you're not to worry about a thing. I've called the doctor.'

'What, our usual doctor?' I asked.

'Oh no,' said Mum, 'Doctor Jasper is some-one we can trust. He knows all about us.'

9.25 a.m.

Dr Jasper was a small gnome-like man with a large, beaming face. 'Ah, here's the young blighter; my, what a pong.' He put on a face mask and then chuckled. 'I can still smell you now, which is a very good sign.'

'Is it?' I asked.

'Oh yes, now open your mouth wide.' He peered through a magnifying glass and then nodded enthusiastically. 'Excellent, excellent – everything is just as it should be. Now, take this immediately.' He handed me a glass with a liquid bubbling away in it.

'Er, what is it?' I asked. 'Something to help me grow up into a nice, big vampire?'

'What a chatterbox you are. Come on, no more questions, down the hatch.'

So I very reluctantly swallowed down this bubbly liquid. It was extremely hot and tasted of absolutely nothing.

'Now,' said Dr Jasper, 'you've had a re-action to this new invader. So you need to be very sick.'

'Oh, great,' I said.

'I know, not very pleasant. But then life is full of little problems and it's no good moaning about them, is it? And right now your body is a battlefield, with your human and vampire sides ranged against each other. But peace will break out – eventually. Well, good morning, Marcus, and with a bit of luck you should be growing fangs tomorrow.'

'So,' I asked Mum later, 'I'm definitely a half-vampire then?'

'Oh, no doubt about it,' said Mum, all happy – in fact, positively gloating.

1.30 p.m.

I've just been very sick – again. Hope that's it now because I don't think I could totter to the bathroom again. I'm totally shattered.

4.00 p.m.

I had just fallen asleep when Mum came in with some more of that foul medicine. 'You know, Mum, I really think I'd rather be doing double maths right now. That should prove how miserable I feel.'

'This is the worst part,' said Mum. 'But it is worth it.'

'Is it really though?' I said. 'Because I've wanted to be a number of things in my life, including a vet, footballer, astronaut and professional chocolate-taster. But I've never for one second wanted to be a vampire or half-vampire or quarter-vampire or even one millionth of one. So is there any way I can stop this and turn back into a normal human being again?'

I suppose it wasn't the most tactful thing I've ever said. But I was ill and stinky and totally fed up.

Mum stopped smiling then all right. And instead she said, 'Your father and I are very proud of being half-vampires. And I hope one day soon, you will be too.'

4.45 p.m.

The doctor has just returned and examined me again. 'You are making excellent progress.' He smiled brightly at me. 'Now, you're going to feel absolutely rotten for the rest of the day. So get some shut-eye if you can. And cheer up . . . because this is a wonderful day.'

'Is it?'

'Yes, because it means the transformation magic has begun.'

6.00 p.m.

Sorry, but too weak to write any more today, blog. Fang tomorrow.

Thursday 4 October
7.45 a.m.

The bad smell has gone – but now my face is itching like crazy. Feel as if I've got chicken-pox, measles and very bad sunburn all at once. I speed to the mirror. And my face is sensationally red – in fact, if it was any redder traffic would stop on it. My eyes are all bloodshot too.

Nestling just inside my top lip is one splendid white fang. I don't expect, blog, you've ever grown a fang. Well, I can tell you, it gives you quite a start. In fact, I couldn't be more shocked if I'd grown another hand. It feels quite solid and strong too. And I keep touching it as if to prove to myself it's real. And it is. It really is. I'm stunned and horrified and oddly proud, all at once. Very, very weird.

Then in pile my parents.

'Oh well, look at that,' cries Mum. 'What a wonderful fang – one of the best I've ever seen.'

'Really!' I can't help feeling a bit pleased. 'You'd say good quality then?'

'For a first fang it's quite outstanding,' says Mum.

'Well, I only grow the best,' I say. 'I mean, a funky guy like me can't go round with an inferior fang.'

And then all three of us start laughing madly. And I'm thinking, For the first time in my life, my parents are actually proud of me. They're positively beaming, in fact.

'Do you mind if we take a picture of you?' asks Dad. 'For the family album we keep in the cellar?'

'I never knew about that secret album,' I say.

'Oh, there's a lot you've got to find out,' says Mum with a merry laugh. 'I know we shouldn't normally talk about this in day-light, but it's such a special occasion.'

Soon Mum is snapping away and I'm even

doing a bit of posing – one boy and his fang –
you know the sort of thing, but actually you
probably don't, do you, blog? Ha, ha.

Then I feel as if I'm about to pass out.

'No, you must stay in bed today – you've
used up all your energy growing that fang,'
says Mum. Then she sighs. 'What a shame
it'll vanish away tonight.'

9.00 a.m.

Dad has just hurled about nine thousand
horror books onto my bed. 'Often far from the
truth,' he said, 'and not to be taken seriously.
But you might enjoy reading about your
ancestry. I've marked all the vampire stories.'

'Funny,' I said. 'Most parents try and stop
their children reading too many horror stories.'

'But then we're not most parents, are we?'
said Dad, chuckling. Both he and Mum are
still in an incredibly good mood.

11.15 a.m.

I've stopped reading already. There's no
getting away from it, vampires are nasty,
bad-tempered, blood-sucking weirdos. And
they're so gloomy all the time. I just want to

say to them, *Lighten up*. I mean, you've never heard of a vampire cracking a joke, have you? While I think laughing is the secret of life. I really do.

Well, think about it – what are the only good bits of school? It's when you're messing about with your mates, isn't it, and you've got a pain from laughing so much. Those funny bits help you get through the rest.

And I'm always messing about, so I'm completely the wrong kind of personality to be a vampire. And yeah, I know I've got a fang dangling down my mouth. But that's nothing to do with me. It's like suddenly catching chickenpox, only I've caught a fang.

I keep examining this fang in my mirror. At first, I'd been a bit excited by what I saw. I even showed off a bit, didn't I? But now I just keep thinking what would happen if someone in my class saw me. They'd run for their life, wouldn't they? Well, maybe not Joel. But even he'd be very uneasy around me. And who could blame him?

I'm just not myself any more. Instead, I'm being turned into a hideous freak. And there's nothing I can do to stop it.

8.35 p.m.

This evening I was allowed to stagger down-stairs. Me and my pet fang sat there watching some telly. And I was trying to feel a bit normal when Dad got up.

'We've got a present for you, Marcus.'

'Bring it on then,' I said.

Dad stepped forward with Mum smiling behind him. 'This is for you, son.' Then he whipped a white envelope out of his pocket and handed it to me.

I looked at it and sniffed. 'Can I smell money inside?' I said.

'Something more precious than that,' replied Dad.

'Hmm, not sure I like the sound of that,' I said, ripping open the envelope. Inside was a card with just one word on it in huge red capitals . . .

VED.

'Say what you see,' asked Dad.

'What is this, an eye test?' I answered. 'I see V E D.'

'Which spells?' asked Dad.

'*Ved*, I suppose.'

Dad and Mum grinned at each other. 'And

we're delighted to inform you,' said Dad, 'that this is your new name, specially chosen for you on your thirteenth birthday by the Half-Vampires Association.'

'Ved!' I exclaimed. 'What a veddy stupid name. This is a joke, isn't it?'

'Don't be silly, love,' said Mum. 'Ved is your true name. And in the evenings when we are alone here or in the company of other half-vampires, we will call you Ved.'

'Oh, please don't,' I cried, 'as I absolutely hate it.'

But Mum and Dad just carried on speaking as though I hadn't said anything. 'It's a fine name,' said Dad.

'Yes, with a wonderful simplicity about it,' added Mum.

This got me even madder. In the end I sprang up and handed Dad the card. 'You like the name so much, you can have it.'

The twinkle which had been in Dad's eye all day suddenly died away. 'Your mother and I already have our half-vampire names, and one day when we think you are ready, you may call us by those names.'

'What a day that'll be,' I said. 'But honestly, pick another envelope; find me a better name than that. How about Brad? I think that sort of suits me.'

'Your name is Ved,' said Dad, getting a bit cross now. 'Honour that name tonight by saying, just before you fall asleep: "I am Ved." Say it now.'

I looked at him. 'I am veddy, veddy sorry, but I hate that name.'

Mum sighed. 'You will come to see that name as a vital part of your ancestry.'

'The day I do that,' I said, 'I won't be me any more. I'll just be some clone of you. And I quite like being me. OK, I'm a bit of an idiot, but basically I'm an all right sort of guy, and that's how I intend to stay.'

Then I stormed upstairs.

9.05 p.m.

Mum and Dad have just visited my bedroom, on a sort of peace mission.

'Overall, we think you're coping very well,' said Mum. 'And your fang will disappear at midnight.'

'So what happens to me next?'

'Cravings,' said Mum.

I gaped at her. 'What!'

'You'll get desperate cravings. You might want to visit graveyards, even try and sleep there,' said Mum.

'Gross or what?' I groaned.

'Oh, it only lasts for a few days,' said Mum airily. 'Well, usually.'

'And what do I do in this graveyard exactly, while I'm having this craving?'

'Oh, just wander about,' said Dad. 'Sometimes you sing too.'

'You have got to be kidding me,' I cried. 'That's tragic.'

'With me,' said Dad, 'I became mad about bats.' He smiled at the memory. 'Spent ages trying to catch one and keep it as a pet.'

'Well, I'm not singing in a graveyard or getting all matey with a gang of bats,' I said firmly.

'Of course, occasionally, half-vampires—' began Dad, but then he saw Mum shaking her head at him and said, 'But no sense in alarming you unnecessarily. I'm sure you won't do that.'

'Do what?' I demanded.

Dad smiled. 'I've said enough – more than the manual recommended, in fact.'

'Well, I can't wait,' I said.

'You won't have to,' said Mum. 'The cravings should start first thing tomorrow. Well, goodnight, Ved.'

'Who's Ved?' I asked. 'Never heard of him.'

'Do me a favour, Ved,' said Dad.

'If you do me one first,' I replied. 'Stop calling me Ved.'

'Ved,' Dad growled, 'I am giving you some important advice, so break the habit of a lifetime and listen. Whatever happens, do not try and stop the vampire side of your nature coming through.'

'No,' said Mum anxiously. 'Never ever do that.'

'Why, what happens then?' I asked. Total silence for a moment. And then I'm sure I glimpsed fear in Mum's eyes.

Fear! But why?

'I know you will be a sensible boy,' Dad said at last, 'and you can start by saying, "I am Ved" over and over. Will you do that for us?'

Total silence from me now.

9.45 p.m.

I've worked out why Mum looked so frightened by my question.

MY PARENTS KNOW I CAN STOP MYSELF FROM TURNING INTO A HALF-VAMPIRE. IT ISN'T A DONE DEAL AT ALL. I STILL HAVE THE POWER TO STAY AS I AM.

And surely I'm entitled to choose. Now, of course, some people – like Tallulah – would love to be half a monster. Actually she'd make a great vampire, as she's got no sense of humour and is always very bad-tempered.

And my mum and dad are obviously having a good time – and that's OK with me. I'm broad-minded.

But it's not for me.

So here's my cunning plan, blog. I shall secretly do everything I can to stop myself from turning into a half-vampire – starting now.

9.55 p.m.

'I am not Ved. I am not Ved.'

I keep chanting this over and over.

10.50 p.m.

'I am not Ved. I am not Ved.'
Yeah, I'm still saying it.

Friday 5 October
3.25 a.m.

Just been woken up by my parents peering at me, with torches. I blinked up at them. 'I'm sure there's a good reason for you two doing this. I'm just not sure I want to hear what it is.'

'Sorry, dear,' said Mum airily. 'We only needed to see if your— Oh, yes, here it is on your pillow.' And she very carefully picked up my white fang. 'We wanted to keep it safe for you.'

'Just make certain you water it every day – and I'll tell you what, why don't you call it Ved?'

'This is for you too,' said Dad, slapping down a five-pound note on my bedside table. 'You get five pounds for a white fang, and guess what you get for your yellow fang . . . fifty pounds!'

'But the yellow fang only comes through,'

said Mum, 'when you have changed over into a half-vampire.'

So that's fifty pounds I'll never see, I thought.

'And don't worry about your cravings tomorrow,' said Mum. 'We'll be here to help you.'

7.05 a.m.

Well, I don't think I've woken up with any wild cravings, but I'll just check with myself:

'Marcus, do you want to leap around singing in a graveyard or pal up with the local bats?'

'Definitely not.'

'And have you got any other cravings?'

'Not one, except – and this is seriously freaky – I want to go to school.'

This has never happened to me before. But right now I want to be back in totally normal, extremely boring, everyday life. I don't even care how mind-rotting the lessons are. Anything's better than hanging out in this Chamber of Horrors.

8.00 a.m.

Mum and Dad were astonished to see me downstairs in full school uniform.

'Oh, we were going to let you have another day off,' said Mum.

'Well, you know I think school's a really groovy place and hate to miss one millisecond.'

They both just stared at me.

'I wonder,' said Mum, 'if it might be wise to wait one more day, until we see how your craving develops?'

'I haven't got a craving,' I said firmly.

'You haven't got one yet,' said Dad eagerly. 'But one could strike during the day.'

'Honestly, I'll be OK,' I said.

And I know I will be.

CHAPTER FOUR

8.50 a.m.

Strolled into my classroom. 'Yeah, folks, start cheering because he's back. And if you've missed me shout "Missed you!" and do it really loudly now.'

Deafening silence.

'Ah well, I guess you're all just too shy,' I said. 'But I can see by your faces how thrilled you are to see me.'

'Of course we're pleased you're back,' came one voice at last: Joel. He started patting me on the back.

'Joel, if I've got just one mate like you,' I said, 'then I really am desperate.'

'So what's been wrong with you?' asked Joel.

'I've had a very rare and mysterious illness,' I said.

'Called skiving,' grinned Joel.

'No, called a severe stomach upset.' I knew this was what my mum had told the school and it wasn't a total lie.

Then I noticed Tallulah hovering by us. I smiled at her.

'Are you looking at me?' she asked.

'Yeah, I suppose I am,' I said.

'Well, don't,' she snapped, and then gave Joel a look before stalking off.

'Don't mind her,' said Joel. 'She's a bit worked up because something's about to kick off.'

'What?' I asked.

'I've sworn an oath of secrecy which stops me divulging the details, even to a fine, upstanding mate like you.' Then he added, 'But you will be truly amazed.'

9.20 a.m.

I have just been 'truly amazed'.

We had Year Eight assembly and Mr

Townley, the headmaster, pranced up onto the stage: bald head, bristly moustache, yappy voice, and wears the same brown suit every single day of his life. He's one of those people who looks cross even when he's in a good mood.

Today he was rattling on about something or other when, bang in the middle of this yawn-fest, Tallulah shot to her feet and shouted out, 'Mr Townley, I want to drink your blood!' Townley's mouth just fell open with shock.

But before he or anyone else could recover, up jumped a boy in my class. 'Mr Townley, I want to drink your blood!' And then another boy and another boy, all chanting the same phrase. Finally up sprang Joel. 'Mr Townley, I want to drink your blood.'

By now, all the mob around me was on their feet – and I thought it would be extremely rude not to join in. So I pranced to my feet and said, 'Mr Townley, I also want to drink your blood. Slurp! Slurp!' I added that last bit just to keep the routine fresh and stop people getting bored.

Well, I got a great bellow of laughter for my

efforts, which pleased me greatly actually.

But Mr Townley suddenly came out of his trance and bellowed, 'Stop this tomfoolery at once.' Although I think it was the highly menacing look in his eyes which also quietened everyone. When Townley goes berserk, even the teachers run for cover.

He then pointed at Tallulah and yelled: 'You, to my room now!' Then he asked the teacher who was hovering beside him like a nervous waitress to take the names of all the pupils who had let down their school so shamelessly. We would all have double detentions, while this assembly would continue after school on Monday, for everyone.

Still, it had been a truly classic moment. I said this to Joel. He agreed with me, but then added, 'Actually, while your enthusiasm was admirable, this was a dare just for the members' – he lowered his voice – 'of the M.I.S.'

'Oh sorry, I hadn't realized this dare was by invitation only,' I said.

'It was an easy mistake to make,' said Joel. 'I'm sure it doesn't really matter.'

11.00 a.m.

Only it did.

I've just had my head torn off by Tallulah. Now there's an experience I'll never forget.

She'd been away from lessons until break time and a rumour went round that she'd been suspended. But she got away with a letter home to her parents – and a double detention. So you'd have thought she might have been a bit relieved about that.

Oh no, she blew over to Joel and me at the end of break like a mad tornado. 'Howlett, you've got the IQ of a plankton,' she cried.

'As high as that!' I cried. 'Oh, thanks.'

'That dare was nothing to do with you, but you had to interfere and try and be funny, didn't you?'

'You didn't like the slurp, slurp bit then?' I said.

'I didn't like any of it,' she cried.

'If I might just interject here,' said Joel. But Tallulah squelched him with a glare. 'Or maybe I'll just stay quiet,' he murmured.

'Because of your act of sabotage,' went on Tallulah, 'all members of M.I.S. have got to do another dare.'

'Oh, have we?' murmured Joel un-enthusiastically.

'Yes we have,' said Tallulah.

'I think sabotage is a bit strong,' I said.

'Nowhere near as strong as a word I'd like to use,' she said.

I said, 'Look, Tallulah, I'm sorry you think I sabotaged your dare, and right now, if I could, I'd make myself invisible.'

'Do it anyway,' said Tallulah. Then she added, 'You don't take anything seriously, but M.I.S. is not to be laughed at, ever.'

As she swept off Joel murmured, 'Isn't she marvellous?'

4.30 p.m.

Now here's a weird thing. When I got home both my parents were waiting for me. But that's not the weird thing yet. No, I'm just building up to that.

They asked me how I was feeling and looked distinctly crestfallen when I said, 'Never better.' They were certain I'd have had some mad cravings by now. Then they asked about my day. So I handed them this letter from Mr Townley saying what a thoroughly naughty boy I'd been.

And normally my parents would have freaked out at receiving a letter like that. But – and here's the weird thing at last – they weren't bothered at all. Well, not when they found out what I'd done in assembly.

'You heard your friends say: "Mr Townley, I want to drink your blood!" and you just had to join in,' said Dad, with pride throbbing in his voice. 'Well, I suppose that's understand-able. You are a half-vampire.'

And there was Mum smiling away too. But that wasn't why I'd joined in. I saw some pupils fooling about and so I had to support them. It was just a laugh and nothing to do with my vampire side bursting through.

4.35 p.m.
Nothing at all. Just like to make that really clear.

4.45 p.m.
Mum said to me, 'So what would you like for tea, Ved?'

'Who are you talking to?' I asked.

'You, of course,' said Mum.

'But my name's Marcus.'

'I'm using your other name – your true name.' And then she said it again really softly: 'Ved.'

'Mum, you really can't do this, you know. After thirteen years of having one name, you can't suddenly give me another one. That's just going to leave me seriously confused. In fact, there's probably a law against it.'

'We wait until your thirteenth birthday to tell you your wonderful secret,' said Mum. 'As that's when we think you're ready to appreciate this news. And it would make your father and me very happy if you would now call yourself by your real name at night, and embrace your destiny,' she said.

'Marcus is my real name,' I said firmly. 'If you really wanted, you could call me Marcus Ved, or Marcus Von Ved – now that's got a certain ring to it, hasn't it?'

Mum just frowned in reply.

10.30 p.m.
'I am not – nor ever will be – Ved.'

I shall fall asleep chanting that again tonight.

Saturday 6 October
9.05 a.m.

It seems to be working. Not a glimmer of a craving. Result, or what?

10.15 p.m.

Tonight Mum said, 'I've got something to show you, Ved.' (Yeah, she and Dad are still pushing that creepy name.) Then she got out her certificate for French A Level. Grade A too.

'Yeah. Great, Mum, but you have let me see it about ninety-four times before. Not that I'm saying you're a show-off or anything.'

'Yes,' she said, 'but did you ever wonder when I found time to study for this exam?'

'Truly, Mum, I never did.'

'It was at night. So while you and millions of other people slept, my half-vampire powers meant I could stay awake and alert for three hours longer than any ordinary human. I'm using my time to study Italian now.'

'I had noticed,' I said, 'how you two seemed to come to bed very late.'

'And soon,' said Dad, 'you needn't go to bed at a normal time either. While all your class-mates are tucked up for the night, you'll be able to stay up with your mother and me until two o'clock in the morning.'

'And even later than that at weekends,' said Mum.

'Wow,' I said. 'So while most children only have to hang out with their parents during the day, I'll be able to stay up half the night with you as well.' I shook my head. 'My friends would be so jealous if they knew.'

Sunday 7 October
10.15 a.m.

Still no sign of any cravings! And the bad breath and the fang now seem far away. In fact, I feel sort of normal again.

7.05 p.m.

Tonight, a surprise visitor! My nan. My parents acted all surprised when they saw her, but I knew at once they'd sent for her.

Now, my mum and dad don't really get me. To them I'm just an idiot. And I know they're secretly a bit ashamed of me. But Nan (my dad's mum) is different. She thinks I'm all right. You can have a laugh with her too. She sat opposite me in one of her gaudy shawls and wearing bright red lipstick as usual. (One of Nan's words of wisdom: 'People always notice you if you're wearing red lipstick.')

'So come on then, Marcus, why are you being such a big nuisance?' she demanded tonight.

'Me? I'm very hurt now,' I said.

She smiled. 'And you never guessed anything before your thirteenth birthday?'

'Not a thing.'

'Well, we're pretty good at keeping secrets. We have to be when it's right at the heart of our lives. And it's an incredible secret, isn't it?'

'You could say that,' I said. Then I lowered my voice. 'I'm not cut out to be a half-vampire.'

'Nonsense,' she said. 'But right now, you're very scared.' I shook my head vigorously. 'Life's not easy for any thirteen-year-old, as I know,' she continued. 'Yes, I can still remember that far back.' We both sort of relaxed and smiled a bit then. 'So teenagers cover up their fears with a lot of cheek and bravado – just like you do.'

'But not many thirteen-year-olds are facing all this stuff,' I said.

'No, they're not,' she agreed. 'Do you know the first thing I did when I heard I was a half-vampire?'

'No.'

'I was so shocked and ashamed I ran away. I jumped on a train actually.'

'I had no idea trains had been invented way back then – that's a joke, by the way. So where did you end up?'

'Oh, somewhere very strange. I didn't have enough money to go home either. So I had to call my parents to come and get me.'

'I bet they were mad,' I said.

'Yes, but they weren't as angry as I expected. They could see why I wanted to run away from it. But that's not the answer. Change is a fact of everyone's life. It's just that our changes are a bit more extreme than most. But, Ved, it's worth it, because there's far more to you than you realize. There really is magic inside you.' She paused. I'd been listening to her really intently. But then she spoiled it all by adding the killer words, 'So come on, Ved, embrace your destiny.'

Not only had she used that horrible name – twice! – but also that's *exactly* what Mum had said: 'Embrace your destiny.' I'm surprised they don't give me a T-shirt with that written on it. But what if you've no intention of embracing your so-called destiny?

So I shook my head and said, 'Good try, Nan, but sorry, no sale.'

10.15 p.m.

Feel more alone than ever tonight, blog. OK, I come from a family of crazies. But that doesn't mean I have to join them.

Nan says: 'There's magic inside you.' What magic? I can stay up late and sit some extra exams. Wow! Spellbinding stuff. And that's the only benefit of being a half-vampire that I can see, while there are tons and tons of drawbacks. Sorry, Nan, I'm chanting 'I am not Ved' even longer tonight.

CHAPTER FIVE

Monday 8 October
8.30 a.m.

Still no cravings! Hooray!

4.15 p.m.
We've just had our after-school assembly with Townley.

He said, 'Today I've discovered that the appalling behaviour in Friday's assembly was the result of a club: the Monster Club, I believe it's called.'

'No, all wrong,' muttered Tallulah.

'Well, I'm telling you,' said Townley, his voice rising, 'that this club stops right now, and anyone still belonging to it at school will face serious consequences.'

Tallulah whispered, 'So now we've got to go underground. Excellent.'

And quite suddenly I grinned. Not for any special reason. I just needed the exercise, I suppose. Only Townley saw me.

'Marcus Howlett,' he screamed. 'Why are you smiling?'

'I'm just enjoying your assembly,' I said. 'One of the best yet. In fact, it's really set me up for the evening.'

Townley didn't know how to react to this. So he waggled his fingers at me and said, 'There are things I will not tolerate. And top of the list is rudeness.'

I stared at him. But I hadn't been rude. A tiny bit sarcastic, perhaps, but not rude.

'I shall be watching you,' Townley went on, while glaring very hard at me. 'I shall be watching you very closely.'

5.20 p.m.

Always when I get home Mum's around. So I was really surprised to find the house empty tonight.

Then I heard a noise in the sitting room.
'Hi,' I called.

No answer.

I barged into the sitting room and got a massive shock. A boy who I'd never seen before was sitting all relaxed and comfortable on our sofa.

'So who are you?' I asked. 'A very lazy burglar?'

'Heard you were a bit of a joker,' said the boy, grinning as he slowly got to his feet. He looked about seventeen, rather scrawny but oozing confidence. He was like a little sparrow strutting about. Only he had jet-black hair and pale staring eyes.

'I'm Karl – Karl with a K not a C, just to clear that up right away.'

'And perhaps you'd also clear up just what you're doing in my house, Karl with a K?'

'Good, like your spirit. It shows potential,' he added approvingly. 'You don't recognize me, do you?'

'I really don't.'

'I'm your second cousin; we met years and years ago at a wedding but only for a few seconds. Anyway, your parents asked me to swing by. I hear you're having a few problems about being a vamp. That's what I call us half-vampires: vamps.'

'And you're a vamp?'

'Crossed over four years ago,' said Karl, giving a little bow. 'I just loved every moment of it. Especially . . . . well, no one in my class could work out why I suddenly wasn't wearing glasses any more.'

'Never heard of contact lenses, had they?' I said.

'My sight just improved so much when I became a half-vampire. In fact, I've probably ended up with the best eyesight of anyone in my school.' Then he gave me the most patronizing smile you've ever seen and said, 'But you're feeling a bit nervous about it all, aren't you? Well, your worries are over because I'm here to help you. First of all, you've got to chill out. And remember, you will never have such an amazing thing happen to you again. So just relax and let out your vamp side, and one day soon you could be exactly like me.'

I tried to look suitably excited at this prospect.

'Your mum and dad have told you about other benefits of being half-vampire: like we only need four or five hours' sleep at night. So at two in the morning I'm still buzzing. But I understand you're worried about the cravings.'

'Well, yeah,' I admitted. 'It sounds . . . messy.'

'And I won't lie to you,' said Karl. 'Cravings can be messy.' He lowered his voice. 'With me it was butchers' shops. Bit of an unusual one, that. And I made a tiny idiot of myself.' He smiled. 'I even got myself banned from my local butcher's shop. But people forget. Well, the butcher still gives me a few funny looks whenever he sees me, but he's very easily frightened.' He grinned at me. 'So have I reassured you?'

'Oh yeah, massively,' I said sarcastically.

'Hey, I told your parents I could sort you out. And here's some more good news. Your mum and dad want us to hang around together, hoping you'll pick up some of my vamp skills, I suppose.' He tried to laugh modestly. 'So that's brilliant, isn't it?'

'Yeah, just wait until my mum and dad

get back,' I said grimly, 'and I can thank them properly.'

5.45 p.m.

'Hey, Mum,' I said, when she finally turned up from wherever she'd been hiding. 'Thanks so much for finding Karl with a K for me.'

And she thought I was being serious. 'Well, it was a bit of luck actually because we'd really lost touch with your Aunt Kate and Uncle Chris as they travel around so much . . .'

'Er, Mum, actually . . .' I began.

But I couldn't stop her burbling on. 'And I knew Karl would be the person to help you – so I wrote to them at the last address I could find for them. Your uncle and aunt are away again, but Karl had to stay behind as he's revising for an exam. And when he read my letter he just sped over here, which is wonderful, as we can't have seen him for years.'

'Mum!' I practically shouted. 'Do me a favour, will you? Send Karl home again now because he's without doubt the most annoying person I've ever met.'

'What's wrong with him?' demanded Mum.

'Where do I start? He's astonishingly big-headed—'

'No, he's not,' interrupted Mum.

'Mum, have you actually spoken to him? He thinks he's the greatest vamp the world has ever seen; also—'

'Oh, honestly, Ved,' interrupted Mum, sounding both exasperated and upset. 'You can be so difficult sometimes. Karl has come a long way just to help you. Can't you be grateful?'

'No.'

'Well, we're all going out tonight.'

'And where exactly are we going?'

Mum hesitated for just a moment. 'We're going to the local graveyard, actually.'

11.30 p.m.

Yeah, that was our cheery destination. It was a very cold night, so the place was deserted, apart from us and a few bats.

'Just feel this wonderful atmosphere,' said Mum. 'It's so peaceful, isn't it?'

'That's because everyone here is *dead*, Mum,' I said. 'So they're not exactly going to be making a racket, are they?'

Dad put a hand on my shoulder. 'Just stop the jokes for a few minutes, Ved. Now, doesn't this place make you feel wonderful?'

'No, sorry, but it really doesn't.' Mum and Dad were so disappointed at this answer that they both had to look away.

'I know what'll change his mind,' said Karl. He slowly and proudly put on his vampire cape. 'I am Count Karl,' he said. 'And I am proud to be a vamp.' Then, before I knew what was happening, he'd put back his head and let out the most gruesome, grisly, blood-tingling howl you've ever heard.

'Now, what about that?' asked Dad.

'I thought it was only werewolves who howled,' I said.

Mum, Dad and Karl all looked very shocked now. 'Werewolves are amateurs compared to us,' said Dad firmly. 'And whenever you hear a strange howling noise in the middle of the night, that's bound to be a half-vampire.'

'You can't hold me back when it comes to howling,' said Karl. 'I practise every single night.'

'Noisy or what?' I said.

'OK, Ved,' said Karl. 'You're looking at me and thinking: I can never be as good at howling as him. And you probably can't. But practice is the key that opens the door of opportunity, so start practising now, Ved.'

'We brought your cape,' said Mum. And she handed it to me, almost shyly.

'Put it on then,' said Dad.

I flung on the cape. Felt so stupid in it, as if I were at a fancy dress or something. But Mum and Dad made 'Oh don't you look smart' noises, and Karl said, 'You'll grow into it in time.'

'Now, just howl as loud as you like,' said Dad.

'Really make our skin crawl,' said Karl. 'You can copy me if you like,' he added.

And I did try. I mean, I didn't want to be a half-vampire. But I wanted to show them – well, Karl mainly – that I could be one of them if I wanted. So I concentrated hard and then out of my mouth came the sound a startled guinea pig might make, only not so scary.

There was a shocked silence. 'That was terrible, wasn't it?' I said.

'You were nervous,' said Mum.

'You need to take a few more deep breaths,' said Dad.

'Maybe I was too good – and put you off?' suggested Karl.

I was determined to do better, so this time I took three very deep breaths, and after each one came a sharp hissing sound. Now I was warmed up and ready to roar. So then I released my second howl. And if a butterfly ever burped – well that's exactly what it would have sounded like.

It was beyond pathetic.

I tottered back in shame. No one spoke. Dad was staring down at a freshly dug grave, looking as if he'd quite like to jump right inside it. Mum had a fixed grin seemingly stuck on to her face.

Finally Karl said, 'I think you're going to need a lot of help, Ved.'

Back home Mum said to me, 'We know you did your best.' I don't think people should ever be allowed to say that, as it only reminds you of how rubbish you've been.

Then Mum left me to read a book about vampires ('It just might help you,' she said hopefully) while she, Dad and Karl whispered in the doorway.

I heard Karl say, 'I've seen vamps as bad as Ved.' And then, after a slight pause, 'No, actually he's the worst vamp I've ever seen.'

Now, I should be pleased by what happened tonight, as I don't want to be a vamp, or anything like Karl. And believe me, I am. But I'm also more than a bit ashamed.

CHAPTER SIX

Tuesday 9 October
12.45 p.m.

All over the school posters have sneaked up saying: 'M.I.S. RULES' and 'I DRINK YOUR BLOOD'. No wonder Townley has been stomping around in a furious mood. But when I congratulated Tallulah she gave me a really icy stare and said, 'I'm waiting for you to try and say something funny now.'

'No jokes at all,' I said. 'Just congratulations.'

She stared at me for a long moment before saying, 'Oh well, thanks.'

4.30 p.m.

Mum's just told me Karl had to rush away to sit his exam. This is the best news I have had for ages. Only he has threatened to return.

Still, I had two more visitors waiting for me tonight – I tell you, I've never had such a busy social life. It was the doctor again. Only this time he'd brought his chum with him: a thin unsmiling woman clutching the biggest clipboard you've ever seen. The moment the doctor started talking she was off, scribbling away.

Mum hovered nervously in the background (Dad was away for the night at a conference) while the doctor said in his breezy way, 'I hear you're having a few problems. Still, we mustn't be down-hearted, must we?' Then he produced a magnifying glass and started peering at me through it. 'Now, I don't want you to worry at all. I'm just going to look into your right eye.'

'I've got a left eye too,' I said. 'In fact, they're what you might call a matching pair.'

'Now, just relax and forget all about me,' he said. Then he started saying weird numbers like C6 and B7 the way dentists do sometimes, while Little Miss Sunshine wrote away furiously on her clipboard.

'No, nothing to worry about there,' he said.

'How are your bowel movements?' asked the woman suddenly, gazing intently at me over the clipboard.

'They're very well, thank you. How are yours?'

'Are you constipated?' she snapped.

'No, my name's Marcus Howlett,' I said. 'And I don't know anyone called constipated. Bit of a strange name really.'

'Stop trying to be funny, dear,' murmured Mum, 'and answer the questions.'

I said, 'OK, my bowel movements are just fantastic – in fact, you can watch them any time you like.'

'Now, young man,' said the doctor, 'remember we're here to help you overcome a few tiny problems. So would you open your mouth and give us a lovely, loud vampire call?'

'What! Here? Now?' I said.

'Yes, please.'

'In front of Miss Clipboard?' I went on.

'Come along now, nice big howl,' urged the doctor.

Well, my heart was thumping as I was still a bit upset about my dismal howling yesterday. And I couldn't believe I was going to do any better in the sitting room with an audience gawping at me.

'Do it, please,' urged Mum.

'Oh, all right,' I said. I closed my eyes and tried. Honestly I did. But I sounded exactly like a field mouse gargling. Then I opened my eyes to see three very depressed faces. 'That wasn't any good, was it?' I said. 'In fact, it was total rubbish.'

The doctor knelt down in front of me. 'Ved,' he said.

'Oh, that's me, isn't it? I keep forgetting.'

'I've examined you carefully and you're as bright as a button, in tip-top health. So the only problem is here inside your head. Your emotions are in a whirl right now. Don't fight the vampire side of you.'

'I'm not,' I said, which I admit was a lie. 'It's just, well, you heard that howl. I haven't got a vampire side.'

'Oh, yes you have,' said the doctor firmly. 'Go on resisting and you're turning your back on your destiny.'

'Wow,' I muttered. 'Big stuff. But answer me this, Doc: what happens if my howl doesn't improve?'

And then something else flashed into his eyes. It came and went so swiftly. But for a moment I'm certain terror looked out at me. He quickly recovered though and said, 'Your howling will improve and those all-important cravings will come. The only block is you: you're choked up with fears and anxieties. So come on, relax and let your special-ness come through.' He stood up. 'Well, I shall look in on you again soon.'

'Groovy – and make sure you bring your friend with you, won't you?' I said, nodding at the woman still writing away on her clip-board. 'As she's great fun.'

10.15 p.m.

Well, the doctor's right about one thing: my emotions are in a whirl. I feel confused and all churned up inside and there's nobody I can talk to about any of this. Not one person – apart from you, blog.

But it comes down to this. I don't want to be a half-vampire and call myself Ved. And surely I should be allowed to choose. No one else.

JUST ME.

Wednesday 10 October
6.05 p.m.

Dad's gone totally mad now. He shouted at me tonight, 'We've been very patient and tried to understand, but enough is enough. Start co-operating – or else, no TV or computer games for a week.'

'By co-operating . . . you mean, what?'

'I think you know,' interrupted Dad. 'It's time you were pulled into line. And that punishment is just the start.'

'Dad, you can't bully me into being a half-vampire, you know.' And I stormed upstairs.

6.35 p.m.

Dad's just called me downstairs. Air was quite dark, I can tell you. And I was ready to say all sorts of stuff, I was so worked up. But instead, Dad stared at the ground and said, 'I'm very sorry for what I said earlier tonight to you. It was wrong. I want to help you, but not like that. Will you please accept my apology?'

'Well, I don't think you'll make that mistake again,' I said. (I've always wanted to say that to an adult.) 'So yes, I will accept your apology.' And then we shook hands for several seconds.

9.50 p.m.

Neither Dad nor Mum has said another word about cravings or half-vampires all evening. I'm not sure why they've suddenly clamped up. They keep whispering away in the kitchen though.

Thursday 11 October
11.15 a.m.

There are stickers in just about every room in the school now saying: 'M.I.S. RULES'. Tallulah has organized this operation really well. And Joel tells me there's now a waiting list of people who want to be M.I.S. members.

8.30 p.m.

Karl is back. He pretended he'd just dropped

by. But really he was here to give me a pep talk. Mum and Dad melted away as soon as he appeared.

He swaggered around the sitting room. 'So what's happening . . . what's new?' he asked. Before I could answer he leaned over me and hissed, 'You still haven't had your cravings?'

'No, I haven't.'

He shook his head. 'And the doctor's called?'

'Oh yeah, he's round here nearly as often as you are,' I said.

'I'm going to be honest with you, Ved,' he said, suddenly stern. 'You're becoming a bit of an embarrassment. In fact, do you know what you remind me of?'

'Amaze me,' I said.

'A little kid who's at the swimming pool and he sees all his mates and his mum and dad in the water, but he can't jump in with them because he's too scared. So he runs around the pool saying, "Ooh, ooh, I don't want to get into the water because I'm frightened." That's how I see you right now.'

'Just one thing,' I said. 'I can swim.'

He paused for a moment. 'Oh, can you?

Yeah, well that's only an example. But you know what I'm saying. Stop being a scaredy-cat and dive in. We've all been very patient with you. But it's time you sorted your head out and crossed over. That's all I'm going to say now. Before I split, I'll leave you with this to think about.'

He let out a howl which I have to admit was truly magnificent. In fact, it could have been in a film.

'I won't ask you to follow that,' he said, 'because I don't want to embarrass you. But one day with a lot of practice you might be nearly as good as me . . . that's something to think about, isn't it?'

Friday 12 October
7.15 p.m.

Told Mum I was going to see Joel. But really I'm off to Brent Woods to practise my howl. I still don't want to be a half-vampire. And I'm very determined about that. But it's bugging me that my howls are so earth-shatteringly terrible.

And if an annoying weasel like Karl can

75

let out ear-piercing howls, surely I can too.

9.30 p.m.

Well, I thumped off to the woods. And there was a low mist so I couldn't see very clearly. Maybe that was why I felt so uneasy. I just had the weirdest feeling that someone was watching me, and not far away either. I even called out once, 'Hey, I can see you.' I couldn't, of course, but the feeling just wouldn't go away. In the end I told myself I was being stupid and I had to concentrate on getting the vampire vibe. I imagined vampires baring their teeth; I heard their snarls ripping through the air . . . And then I let out a howl a budgie might make when it wants its water changing.

Truly pathetic.

And right after my effort came loud, mocking laughter.

I whirled round and cried, 'Who dares to laugh at me?'

Out of the mist stepped Tallulah.

'How rude,' I said. 'Eavesdropping on a private howl – and then laughing.'

'That wasn't just bad—' she began.

'I did hear it too,' I interrupted, 'and will admit that wasn't one of my finest efforts.'

She edged closer to me. 'Why are you out here making howling noises anyway?'

I hesitated. How could I explain this? Finally I said very quickly, 'Well, monsters are the big thing in our school now, thanks to you. And my best mate Joel's joined the M.I.S. and I suppose I'd kind of like to join too.' Yes, I was lying my head off, but I had to say something, didn't I? And Tallulah was believing me – sort of.

'You?' She laughed.

'Yes, me.'

'You want to join M.I.S.? But you're a total idiot.'

'Ah, there's another side to me entirely. And I thought if I could perform a really incredible vampire howl, you'd see me in a whole new light.'

'Highly unlikely . . . still, I'm glad you picked a vampire to try and impersonate as they're the best monsters of all.'

'They're certainly the meanest. Even when they're being a bit suave and welcoming people to their castle they're plotting to unleash major nastiness.'

She smiled fondly. 'I know they really shake things up. They're total anarchists like me.'

'So what are you doing here?' I asked.

She looked surprised by my question. 'I come here just about every night to think up new monster stories.'

'Every night?' I echoed disbelievingly.

'Horror is what I do. It's my life.'

'But isn't it a bit . . . well, lonely?'

'You're never alone if you've got horror in your blood.'

'And your parents don't mind?'

'No, they're really pleased to get rid of me, as I have nothing in common with them. Not one single thing. Well, you know where they all are tonight – watching my little sister at majorettes. She's been training for weeks to prance about twirling batons – and they think *I'm* weird.'

'Have you just got one sister?'

'Yeah, but I've got an older brother as well – unfortunately. He's perfect too, of course. In fact, my family's a little pack of perfection, all

living on the Planet Bland. And there's me
. . . me the joke, the freak, me the . . . the . . .'
Suddenly she was so angry she could hardly
talk. 'But why are we wasting time talking
about them?' she asked sternly. 'They're
nothing to me. Let's hear you do a proper
vampire howl now.'

'You're going to stay and listen?' I said.

'Of course,' she snapped.

I closed my eyes and muttered, 'Here goes
nothing,' and tried again. 'That was a bit
better, wasn't it?' I said hopefully.

'Last time,' said Tallulah, 'your roar
sounded like the noise a little worm might
make.'

'And this time?' I asked.

'This time you sounded like quite a big
worm.'

'And what are my chances of going any
higher up the evolutionary scale?'

'Very slight,' she said.

'I love the way you spare my feelings.'

She shook her head. 'I just don't think
you've got any horror in your blood.'

'You'd be surprised,' I murmured.

'What's that?'

'Nothing,' I said quickly. 'So there's no chance of me joining Monsters in School then?'

'Absolutely none right now,' she said. 'Our standards are very high though.' Then she added unexpectedly, 'But keep practising.'

Saturday 13 October
9.00 p.m.

You know how the air feels thick and heavy just before a massive thunderstorm breaks out? Well, that's exactly how my house feels tonight. A very strange atmosphere, just as if something's about to happen. Something big.

Sunday 14 October
11.30 p.m.

It's happened.

CHAPTER SEVEN

Sunday 14 October
11.33 p.m.

Earlier, I'd fallen asleep surprisingly quickly. I think I just wanted to get today over with. But then I jumped awake. I'd heard something, a kind of rustling sound as if a bird had flown in here by mistake. And now it was roosting right in the darkest, most shadowy part of my room.

How could a bird get in here? That was nonsense. Something was here though. I was sure of it. I was surprisingly calm about it too. Maybe because I was still only half awake.

I leaned forward. 'Er, hey,' I called. Don't

ask me why I said that. I certainly never expected a reply. But that's exactly what happened.

A voice said, 'Now, don't be afraid, everything will be all right.'

A voice I recognized instantly. 'Dad, where are you – look, I'm going to put a light on.'

'No, don't do that,' said Dad, so fiercely I froze.

Nothing happened for a moment, except my whole room sort of shivered. And then something came flapping out of the shadows. Only it wasn't a bird.

It was a bat. The biggest one I'd ever seen. It swirled and whirled above my head – and came tumbling out of the air and straight towards me. For a second I saw the flash of burning red eyes and then it landed on my neck. It felt surprisingly soft and furry. But I really didn't want it hanging onto me.

'Dad,' I called. Where was he when I needed him? 'Get this thing off me, will you?'

Dad didn't say a word. In fact, the only sound I heard was a kind of slurping noise. The bat obviously thought it was feeding time. I tried to pull it off my neck, but suddenly it was as if all my energy was being sucked away. I couldn't even move my arm. In fact, I could hardly even speak.

'Dad, help . . . help,' I stuttered.

I must have passed out then, but only for a few seconds, because when I came to again, the bat was still there. It was hovering just over my head as if getting ready for another feast. I could hear its breath hissing slightly and on its mouth were beads of bright red blood: *my* blood.

I was so angry now that I found the energy to snarl, 'This restaurant is closed, so don't you dare come flapping near me again.'

And instantly the bat vanished. It was as if I'd chanted a magic spell. I couldn't believe it. And instead there was just my dad leaning over me and looking all concerned.

'Dad, there was this bat . . .' I began. 'And it . . .' But my voice fell away. I gazed up at my dad in total horror. Tiny specks of blood were there on his lips now.

'That bat was *you*,' I cried, 'wasn't it?'

'I'm very sorry, Ved,' said Dad, wiping his lips with his hankie. 'But you see . . .' He hesitated.

'Yes?'

'I had to blood you.'

'Blood me?' I yelled. I thought he'd gone crazy. Yes, all parents were weird but mine really were total loonies. I tried to get out of bed.

'No, don't move yet.'

But I ignored this and stumbled to my feet. I wanted to see what had happened to me. I tried to look at myself in the mirror, only it was like staring at a faulty telly. And I couldn't see myself properly at all. One second I was there, the next I'd completely vanished. I wasn't moving but my reflection was jumping about all over the place.

'What's happening to me?'

'It's all right, love, it's only temporary,' said Mum, who'd appeared in the doorway. 'It's normal at this time to have a little trouble with your reflection.'

'Normal?' I practically shrieked. 'Nothing's normal in this house. But this is creepy on a whole new level. Look, what's going on here?'

'Ved, come back to bed,' said Mum. 'You're bound to be very confused and—'

'After my dad turns into a vampire bat and

attacks me – yeah, to be honest, that was a tiny bit of a shock,' I began. I had more to say, but then my legs buckled and I had to be helped back into bed by Mum and Dad.

'Now, just lie quietly,' said Mum.

'Why, what have you got planned for me next? If you could warn me when you're planning to turn into another blood-seeking creature, I'd be very grateful.'

'Look, will you just let me explain?' said Dad. 'I never knew a boy like you for making a fuss.'

'Oh, I'm sorry,' I began, 'but I've just been attacked.'

'No, you haven't,' said Dad quite snappily.

'Please let your father explain,' said Mum. 'He's been on edge all day about this.'

I gazed up at Dad. 'Go on then, explain.'

Dad sat down on the bed. 'You've heard of the flu jab, haven't you?'

'Yes,' I said cautiously.

'Certain people have that to protect them. People who might be at special risk from flu.'

'You're not telling me that was the flu jab you gave me tonight,' I said.

'No,' replied Dad. 'It was the vampire jab.'

I nearly laughed. 'What?'

'You are having a few little problems in changing over into a half-vampire. The jab tonight just helps to accelerate the process.'

'It stops me having a choice, you mean,' I said. 'Look, I don't want to be a half-vampire. Sorry, but I'm just not into vampires. You're forcing me to be like you.'

'No,' said Dad. 'That's not how it is.'

'Actually, Dad, that's *exactly* how it is. And you giving me the vampire jab is a bit of a giveaway.'

'Please believe us,' said Mum. 'We did this for your own safety.'

'Oh yeah, sure. I ought to report the pair of you to Childline,' I said. 'Not to mention the European Court of Human and Half-Human Rights. I'm sure they'd like to be in on this too. And yeah, they might find the story a bit far-fetched at first, but I suppose there's the little tell-tale sign on my neck. That's my proof, isn't it?'

Dad didn't answer. Instead, he walked out.

'Oh, you've really upset him now,' said Mum.

'I've upset him?' I asked. 'Look at *me*.'

'You'll just feel a little under the weather for an hour or two,' said Mum. 'And your neck might be a bit itchy. So try and not scratch it as that will wear off very soon and tomorrow morning you'll feel as right as rain again.'

'But something's happened to me tonight, hasn't it?'

'Yes,' said Mum. 'But you've got to trust us; it's for your own good.' She smiled at me. 'Now, do you trust us?'

'Sorry, Mum, but right now I really don't.'

There was a little catch in Mum's voice as she said, 'Well then, I don't know what to say, except if you can't trust us we've obviously failed you. So it's all our fault.' With that she left too.

11.50 p.m.

Parents have no right turning themselves into bats. It's just not what you expect from them. Yet after all that carry-on I'm now supposed to feel sorry for them!

11.55 p.m.

Crept to the top of the stairs. Mum sounds really upset now – and Dad's comforting her by saying, 'The vampire jab had to be done. Everyone we asked said that.'

11.57 p.m.

The vampire jab – have you ever heard anything dafter? I think my mum's crying now. Well, how dare she! No one attacked her. 'We're doing our best,' she sobbed. 'Why can't Ved see that?'

Because I'm not Ved, for a start. But Marcus or Ved, I can't sit up here listening to my mum crying for another second. She obviously thinks she's helping me. They both do. And that's got to count for something, I suppose. And if you can't trust your parents . . . Somehow I've got to trust them.

12.30 a.m.

I shuffled downstairs – my legs felt like cotton wool. And Mum rushed over, hugging and kissing me and saying, 'We only did this tonight because we want the best for you.'

I could have argued this one, but I didn't. Instead, I let Mum and Dad help me onto the couch, after which Mum sped off to make me some tea. There was a slightly awkward silence then, until I burst out, 'Well, what do you know, I've got a dad who can turn himself into a bat, and pretty speedily too. How long does it take you?'

'About twenty seconds.'

'Wow, is that a world record or anything? Because it should be.'

'It's a good time,' said Dad modestly. 'I thought a long time before I gave you that vampire jab,' he went on. 'I even went off on a little training course—'

'When you were supposed to be at a conference,' I interrupted.

'That's right. I wanted to make sure I did it exactly right. And what you've got to believe is that it was done for your safety.'

'There you go with that safety stuff again,' I said. 'Can you just explain that?'

Dad hesitated. 'Let's just say we want this changeover to happen as quickly as possible, for your sake. Now, no more questions tonight.'

'Well, just one more – will I ever be able to turn into a bat?'

'Once the changeover is complete you will,' said Mum, coming in with the tea. 'And one night the three of us will be able to go flying off together. We're so looking forward to that.'

'There's nothing more refreshing,' added Dad, 'than a late-night flit.'

He made it sound so normal – like going off to a football match or something. And I'd kind of like to go for a late-night flit – just for the experience. Well, it'd be great, wouldn't it?

But nothing else about being a half-vampire floats my boat. Not one single thing.

Monday 15 October
7.45 a.m.

First thing I noticed when I woke up was that the itch on my neck had stopped. I scrambled out of bed. My reflection was back inside the mirror again. I looked terrible, with my hair sticking up everywhere. But there was no sign I'd received the vampire jab except for a tiny mark on the left side of my neck. It seemed just like a little mosquito bite; nothing unusual at all.

8.25 a.m.

Downstairs, everything was just as normal

too. In fact, last night seemed as far away as a dream. I sensed Mum and Dad didn't want to talk about it either – not that they're keen to chat about vampire stuff in the daytime anyway. So they just waffled on about what was in the newspaper and what time Dad would be home tonight.

'Hope you have a peaceful day, love,' said Mum to me. 'And if anything happens I'll be at home all day,' she went on.

'What do you mean?' I asked.

'Stop worrying the boy,' said Dad. 'He'll be fine.'

'Yeah, I've had my jab. What can happen to me now?'

Neither Mum nor Dad smiled.

'Not a word about that at school,' said Dad.

'Oh, of course not,' I said. 'No one would believe me anyway.'

12.45 p.m.

Despite what you may have heard, I've never done anything totally disgusting and sick – until now.

It happened out of the blue as well, at the end of morning lessons, when Joel got a

91

nosebleed. He has these really bad ones too, like little explosions. So he was sent to Matron's cave and, as I'm his best mate, I accompanied him.

Joel had to walk with his head well back as he was getting through about four hankies a second. I was guiding him, saying, 'Next time have your nosebleeds a bit earlier, will you, as we're only going to miss the last four minutes of lessons, which is nowhere near enough.'

Joel gave a sort of gurgled laugh in reply.

Then we finally rolled up at Matron's. Nearby also lurk the school secretary, the deputy head, and the head himself. That's why it is, without doubt, the gloomiest part of the whole school.

I knocked on Matron's door. It just flew open. This large woman with a squashed nose and an amazing collection of chins glared suspiciously at us. She absolutely hates being disturbed – especially by pupils. 'Nosebleed,' she snapped at Joel, her eyes bulging disapprovingly at having her day interrupted like this. 'All right, you in here and you' (meaning me) 'back to your classroom immediately.' She boomed that last word as the door crashed shut.

It was then I noticed it.

One of Joel's handkerchiefs had fallen to the ground. So I picked it up. It was just sopping with fresh blood. I looked around. No one was about. So then I had the maddest, silliest impulse of my whole life. And I started squeezing the blood into my cupped hand. Then my stomach started to rumble.

In fact, I'd never felt hungrier in my life. It was as if I hadn't eaten for days. That's why, without another thought, I started to slurp up Joel's blood. I ran it about in my mouth for a moment and then I swallowed it down; warm, soft and just bursting with flavours. I've never tasted anything so delicious in my whole life.

Then I remembered Joel had flung his large hankies into the bin outside Matron's office. I quickly scooped them up and then let this lovely fresh blood gush down my throat too.

But it still wasn't enough. I had to have more. More! And who knows where I'd have gone shuffling off to next if the bell hadn't rung. And that was like an alarm waking me up from a terrible dream.

What was I doing licking up all that blood like a . . . a VAMPIRE? What I'd just done was SICK, DISGUSTING! I was so angry I put back my head and let out a loud howl. It seemed to happen without me making any effort at all. The howl just ripped through me. And I sounded like a poodle who'd forgotten where he'd buried his dog biscuits and was just furious about it.

So no, I still wasn't very menacing, but I'd certainly acquired some volume. That was by far my loudest howl so far. Although right outside Matron's office and with the headmaster's den just two doors away perhaps wasn't the best location for such a sound effect.

And then quite a few things happened at once. First of all, Tallulah came rushing up to me.

'Was that you howling?' she cried.

'Er . . . yes,' I said hoarsely. 'It was, actually.'

'That was better.'

'Thanks.'

'Still very poor, but louder,' she said. 'It lacked any authentic horror though. Still, to do it here of all places – respect for that.' And a smile even flickered briefly across her face, which was kind of cheering. It was just a shame I also had to edge briskly away from her as I stank – of blood. Next, Matron burst out of her room and bellowed, 'Marcus, did you just make that appalling sound outside my door?'

I swallowed hard. 'Do you know, I think I must have gone into a little trance there for a few seconds as I have no memory of what I just did. You think I made a howling noise? Well, how odd. Could you describe it to me at all?'

'What nonsense are you babbling now?' demanded Matron. 'I'm sending you to the headmaster.' But there was no need as he had already come striding out of his lair to see what was going on.

When he saw me he groaned. 'If ever there's trouble, you're not far away.' And then I was swiftly marched into his torture chamber, only able to glance briefly at Tallulah, who was smiling at me for a second record-breaking time.

My interview with the headmaster was short and not at all sweet. He assumed I'd let out that howl as a monster dare. I didn't argue as I just wanted to get out of there and clean myself up. So he waggled his ferocious eyebrows about and gave me four detentions and I said, 'Thank you very much indeed.' After which he gave me a very funny look and I left.

I sped to the nearest loo next, which luckily was empty, and gave my face and hands a thorough wash. Then I gargled with water to clean my mouth out.

My craving for blood had gone – for now.

CHAPTER EIGHT

Monday 15 October
3.00 p.m.

'I was in Matron's office,' said Joel, 'with her looming over me and my nosebleed still in full flow when your howl just erupted into the room. And Matron leaped right up into the air as if someone had just stuck a pin up her backside. "What was that?" she screeched, all her chins wobbling together, like a giant concertina. I tell you, mate, right then I felt so glad to be alive, and as for my nosebleed . . . it had totally stopped.'

'You're kidding me,' I cried.

He started to laugh. 'And you know what, I'd say it was your howl which cured me. You're not a witch doctor, are you?'

'You'd be surprised,' I said.

3.55 p.m.

I was just walking out of school with Joel when Tallulah rushed up to us. 'What are you doing on Thursday night?' she asked me.

'Well, I haven't got the seven volumes of my social diary with me, but at a rough guess I'd say – absolutely nothing.'

'Well, you are now,' she said.

Joel stared at her. 'Hey, you're not asking him out for a date, are you?'

She made very loud throwing-up noises and then said, 'You really want to join Monsters in School, don't you, Marcus? That's why you made that improved but still hideously mediocre howl today, isn't it?'

Actually I had no interest in joining M.I.S. at all. Well, as I keep telling you, blog, I don't even like horror stories very much. But I still replied, 'Ah, you know all about me, don't you?'

'Yes, I do,' said Tallulah. 'And I can't let you come along as a member, but you can attend the next meeting on Thursday – as a visitor.

I will tell you our secret meeting place nearer the time. But I'm giving you a task now: on Thursday night you must tell a story which terrifies everyone. It needn't be very long, just make sure it's really horrible. Do that successfully, and who knows?'

Before I could reply she'd strode off. She always acts as if she's in a terrible hurry. And Joel let out a loud sigh of amazement. 'What a day this has been. But is that right? You did that howl because you wanted to be in the M.I.S.? Or maybe,' he added with a teasing smile, 'it's Countess Tallulah you like.' Then he darted off before I could punch him.

4.20 p.m.

At home, and Dad is back early. He and Mum look up very expectantly as I walk in. I give a little bow. 'The craving has landed. But you guessed that. I mean, the so-called vampire jab gave me no choice, did it?'

'It speeded up things, yes,' said Dad.

'But what is the craving?' asked Mum.

'Would you believe *blood*? Sorry I can't be more original.' Then I filled them in on the day's grisly events. And when I finished neither of them could stop these little smiles breaking out on their faces.

'So tell me,' I said, 'when does my next blood craving kick in? Or is that to be a wonderful surprise?'

'You usually get really intense cravings about twice a day,' said Mum.

'You say this like it's a good thing,' I said.

'It is,' said Mum quietly.

'Mum, I'm drinking blood. I'm a gory freak.'

'No,' Mum and Dad protested together.

'Oh, I know for you two it's a sign I'm the chosen one, and the more blood I slurp, the prouder you'll be. But I'm hating every disgusting second. So how long will all this fun go on for anyway?'

'Only usually about three or four days,' said Mum. 'And don't worry, we'll look after you.' Her voice was all soft and concerned, but she couldn't stop another smile from forming. A smile of victory, I thought angrily. I was turning into one of them.

'So does this craving mean I'm now officially a half-vampire?'

'Oh, no,' said Dad. 'You've got lots to do yet.'

'Will you be giving me another jab for that, then?' I asked.

'No,' said Dad firmly. 'No more jabs. The rest of the transformation into a half-vampire has to come from you.'

So that was one little bit of good news, I suppose.

7.05 p.m.

Just had an almost raw steak, swimming in blood, all of which I lapped up. I tell you, when you're drinking blood it just glides down your throat so effortlessly. I suppose there's a very faint blackcurrant flavour, but it's stronger and much juicer than that. And it's very, very more-ish. No, really . . . I guess you're just going to have to trust me on this one.

After I'd finished I gave a little contented sigh and Mum said proudly, 'Well, that should keep you ticking over for a while.'

7.45 p.m.

Ticking over as a half-vampire. Now the revulsion is kicking in again as I realize I'm turning into something that just isn't me.

9.30 p.m.

Dad said he's very proud of me today. For what, exactly? Gulping down blood?

10.40 p.m.

My parents haven't won yet. I can still stop this.

'I don't want to be a half-vampire. I don't want to be a half-vampire.' Never have I said this more urgently.

**Tuesday 16 October
7.50 a.m.**

My parents told me I needn't go to school today – give my cravings a chance to settle down. But I didn't want to stay here all day. So I turned down their kind offer.

11.45 a.m.

Nearly lunch time – most people are starting to think about food. But I can only think of one thing: blood.

12.05 p.m.

Feeling dizzy with craving now. In fact, I can

hardly even hear what anyone is saying. I shall have to slip out of school and get blood from somewhere.

12.15 p.m.
Lunch time and a message from Mum. She wants to see me urgently in reception.

12.25 p.m.
Mum sees me and calls out loudly, 'You silly boy, you went off today without your lunch box.' Actually I don't have a lunch box, but I gabble thanks, and then tear off to the back field.

Inside there are steak sandwiches absolutely bursting with blood. I pile them into my mouth, letting the blood ooze down my throat. Never has anything tasted better in my whole life.

Wednesday 17 October
12.30 p.m.

Just had another blood craving. But today I had a fresh supply of blood sandwiches in my tuck box.

Blood sandwiches – I tell you, you just can't beat them.

1.05 p.m.
But as soon as the craving is over I hate myself; even though it's not really me acting like this. It's as if I've been put under a spell.

4.15 p.m.
After school, Joel said all mysteriously, 'Don't go home just yet.' He led me down this little alleyway near our school. Tallulah was waiting for me and looking so serious I just wanted to laugh.

She handed me a folded-up card. 'This tells you where we're meeting tomorrow. After you've read it—'

'Eat it,' I interrupted.

'Are you going to keep being stupid?' she snapped.

'Probably, yeah,' I said.

'If you don't take it seriously,' she said, 'you'll be chucked out of M.I.S. before you've even joined and have to go back to your very boring, very dull life.'

Now, my life is a lot of things right at the moment, but very boring and very dull definitely aren't two of them. I didn't argue though; instead I said very respectfully, 'So to check, I don't eat the card.'

'No, you just destroy it,' she snapped.

'Before or after I've read it?' I asked.

'I thought you were trying to be sensible,' she sighed.

'And he is,' cut in Joel.

'Just one more question,' I said. 'Wouldn't it have been easier if Joel had just told me where we were meeting?'

'No, it wouldn't,' she practically shouted. And Joel shook his head at me in a 'Do keep your mouth shut' sort of way. Tallulah continued, 'That card also contains tonight's password, and of course no one will be admitted who's not wearing a monster mask.'

'Now that could be a little problem,' I said, 'as I haven't got any masks at home.'

She stared at me as if I'd just said I hadn't got a bed in my house. 'Joel, sort him out, will you?' Then she added, 'And I hope your horror story is very scary. Otherwise you'll have no chance of ever joining M.I.S.'

Then she was gone and Joel said, 'Do you want to try your horror story on me?'

'I would,' I replied, 'but I haven't thought one up yet.'

Thursday 18 October
5.30 p.m.

Dear blog, please read the next few lines and then immediately eat them. For here are the top-secret details of the M.I.S. meeting.

It's at the cricket pavilion (wonder how Tallulah got us in there) at 8.00 p.m. and tonight's secret knock is – three knocks very fast. The password is: 'I'm a blood-sucking maniac.' That should make me feel right at home!

See you there.

6.10 p.m.

Do you know who can wind me up more than anyone else, yeah, even more than Karl? MY PARENTS. You won't believe what they've just said now.

I mentioned to them, ever so casually, that I was going out tonight. Dad immediately said, 'What about your homework?'

'Oh, didn't you hear?' I replied, 'I'm not allowed to do homework on account of me having a photographic memory. The teachers say it really puts the other pupils off.' Mum and Dad actually smiled at this and I added, 'Honestly, I really have done all my homework tonight,' and got up to get ready.

Then Dad said, 'I'm sorry, but we still don't want you going out tonight. It's too risky.'

'I'll be home by ten o'clock though – maybe earlier, if Tallulah chucks me out of Monsters in School – and you liked me joining this.'

'No, I'm sorry,' said Dad again. 'It's totally out of the question. You're not going out right now.'

Well, I got really angry then and said, 'I've had a totally miserable time lately, what with growing fangs and slurping up blood and putting up with Cousin Karl – and all because of your lousy genetics. But now I just want to go out for a couple of hours with my mates and you won't let me. Come on, reconsider, please.'

Now any decent parent would have relented and said, 'Actually, Marcus' (or Ved as they still persist in calling me) 'you've put up with a lot lately and deserve a little break with your mates, so yes, go away and enjoy yourself.'

But Dad didn't relent. And Mum looked away when I tried appealing to her.

So I'm under house arrest until they decide otherwise.

Well, I'm about to show my parents they can't boss me around.

CHAPTER NINE

7.40 p.m.

I'm out.

And the prison guards haven't even realized – yet. Mum and Dad were at the front door talking to a neighbour who was collecting for something (and my parents just told me how they always make a big deal of being 'in' with the neighbours so they'll think we're a totally normal family).

So I saw my chance and slipped out of the back door and called for Joel as planned. He was already wearing a zombie mask and said, 'So what do you want: a werewolf or vampire mask?'

'Vampire,' I said at once. I couldn't help

feeling a certain family loyalty, despite everything.

'Good choice,' said Joel. 'I nearly chose that one too but I saw *Shaun of the Dead* again last night – and there's no denying that zombies have a charm all of their own.'

We cut through Brent Woods. The air had a chill to it and a dark, damp mist was rolling in. 'Just the right weather for a M.I.S. meeting,' said Joel cheerfully. 'And do me a favour tonight, mate.'

'What's that?' I asked.

'However weird Tallulah gets . . . don't try and make me laugh.' Of course we both immediately started rolling about laughing. 'No, come on,' said Joel, 'serious face now, and we can kill ourselves laughing at her afterwards.'

As we left Brent Woods, the common stretched ahead of us and beyond that was the cricket pavilion. 'So how did Tallulah get permission to use this?' I asked.

'She didn't,' said Joel. 'She said it would be lying empty until the spring so she just broke in.'

We did the secret knock, said the password

and then the door edged open very slowly. It was quite dark inside, save for a couple of candles flickering away. Spiders and bats hung down from the ceiling as, very weirdly, did some small coffins. There were fold-up chairs stacked in the corner but no one was sitting down. Instead, everyone was standing around in their masks holding bright-red drinks in little paper cups.

'This is like a cocktail party for freaks,' I whispered to Joel.

'You should feel right at home then,' he whispered back, 'and remember, don't say anything at all funny – or you'll get us both chucked out. Now, drink up your blood.'

'What are you talking about?' I cried, startled.

'The glass of blood you're holding in your hot little hand, of course,' said Joel. 'What did you think I meant?'

Of course, it wasn't blood. It was a fizzy lemonade-style drink. Only it did look a tiny bit like blood. And I thought, What a shame it isn't the real thing.

That idea just popped into my head. But immediately I was alarmed. Was I getting another craving? No, I'd had my quota for today – two. There was no chance of any more, was there? I couldn't be sure though. Maybe the cravings were going to get worse tonight. Was that why my parents weren't letting me out? Did they know something they hadn't told me? It is decreed on the fourth day that the cravings will multiply?

What if I had another mad thirst here? What if I suddenly attacked someone – leaped onto their neck and let my teeth sink into . . . ? NO, NO, NO. I was thinking total rubbish. I'D NEVER LET MYSELF DO THAT.

Then Tallulah, wearing a vampire mask quite similar to the one I'd borrowed from Joel, took a chair and sat down on it. Everyone gathered around her on the floor. She gazed down at us like some VIP vampire and said, 'Ghouls, welcome to the dark side. Tonight we have a possible new member.'

'Hi, everyone,' I said. 'And it's great to be with so many creeps – I mean creepy people.'

Tallulah said, 'Your task . . . your first task—'

'Excuse me, but how many tasks will I have to do?' I interrupted.

'It depends,' said Tallulah.

'On what?' I asked.

'On me, mainly,' she said. 'Now, your first task is to tell us a story filled with blood-chilled terror. Good luck,' she added.

'Thanks a million. Well, it's great to be here at Ghouls Towers . . . it really is.' Then I smiled nervously. The truth was, I still hadn't properly thought out what I was going to say. No, I'd been far too busy drinking blood and arguing with my parents. Joel had given me a few suggestions on the way here, but they'd all vanished from my head.

Nine masked faces peered at me expectantly.

'It was a dark and gloomy night,' I began.

'Boring,' muttered a zombie.

'No heckling, please,' I said, 'or I'll forget where I was . . .'

'It was a dark and gloomy night,' prompted Tallulah.

'Thanks, and it sure was. A bit like tonight actually, where there's a thick mist creeping in and out between the trees.'

'Oooh, I'm so scared,' called a mocking voice.

'Just be patient,' I began. Then I decided to be honest. 'The thing is, although this story was a major priority, I've had a few problems at home.'

Someone started to sob loudly.

'All right, spare me the sarcasm,' I said. 'So I wondered if I could have a bit more time – I promise you all that I'll have such a brilliant tale to tell you for the next meeting.'

'No, you've got to tell it tonight,' said Tallulah firmly. 'That was the deal, but you can hear a few more stories first, which might give you some ideas. I will start.' She lowered her voice. 'His head fell forward to the ground, covered in blood. A look of mortal terror was frozen on his dead face . . .'

And that was the most cheerful part of her story. How could I possibly match that?

9.15 p.m.

Something TRULY TERRIBLE has just happened.

I was waiting to tell my story, and pizza was being passed around and it was – although Tallulah would kill me for saying this – kind of cosy sitting there hearing ghoulish tales.

So I sat there enjoying a huge slice of pizza. Funny, it was one thing we'd never had at our house. But it was really tasty. Meatball Feast, it was called. And I'll never forget that name!

Then it was my turn to tell a story again. 'Right, well, there had been thunder and lightning all night.'

'All night – that's impossible,' called out a voice.

'Not in my story, it isn't. You see, this is set in the future—'

'How far in the future?' asked someone.

'Well, if you'll stop interrupting I'll tell you. I can't say a line without someone butting in. Now—' And I let out a really husky gasp.

'Good sound effect,' said a voice.

Only it wasn't, because my throat felt as if it had suddenly burst into flames: it was scorching me. I started to cough. 'Water,' I quavered and then my voice just died out.

Joel got up and grabbed, not water, but that red drink we'd all had earlier.

'Stop fooling about,' said an angry voice.

'He's not,' said Joel, pouring some of the red

liquid down my burning hot throat. 'I can tell.'

'Both his ears have gone bright red,' said someone else.

Tallulah had got up from her throne and half whispered to me, 'What's the matter?'

I couldn't answer. All I could do was make this weird wheezing sound. I was very embarrassed and very, very scared. What was happening to me?

'Air,' I managed to gasp at last. I stumbled for the door but then my legs buckled. Joel had to half carry me outside. Everyone else followed.

'It's all right, he doesn't want to have an audience,' said Tallulah. 'Come back inside when you can,' she said to me and they all returned inside the pavilion, except Joel and me.

'You'll be all right,' said Joel. 'That pizza was quite strong – especially the garlic sausage.'

For a second I stopped coughing. I nearly stopped breathing. Garlic – but that's extremely bad for vampires, isn't it? It's like their deadliest enemy and I'd just eaten a great chunk of garlic sausage. What was going to happen to me now? Was I suddenly going to start decomposing? Well, if so that was something I really wanted to do alone, as decomposing is a very private activity, isn't it? So I said, 'I'll be all right, Joel, you go back, I'm going home.'

'But you can't go on your own, not in the state you're in,' Joel replied.

'No, no, I don't want to ruin your night,' I stuttered. 'I'll be fine.' And from somewhere I found the energy to run. I raced away from Joel just as fast I could.

But he came after me calling my name really loudly and saying, 'Don't be silly, mate. I'll see you home.'

He's a surprisingly fast runner too and would soon catch up. But in the end I managed to get away from him and climb up a tree. Then I wriggled my way along a wide branch.

And that's where I am now, waiting to see what happens to me next.

CHAPTER TEN

Friday 19 October
9.45 a.m.

Sorry, blog, not to have been in contact any earlier. But so much has happened to me since my last correspondence – at the top of that tree.

I sat up in the tree for ages and ages, actually. I still had a really bad case of the gripes. But that's all. I hadn't crumbled away to dust or anything. So that was a bit of good news, I suppose. And feeling surprisingly cheerful, I finally clambered down the tree and decided to stagger home.

The mist seemed to hang over everything now. In fact, I thought if I stood still long enough it would start wrapping itself over me. So I stumbled forward, not quite sure where I was going.

The woods were deathly quiet too, as if everything had gone into a trance. But through the mist I could hear the odd noise like birds rustling and shifting about in the trees.

And then I heard something else: the sound of a human crunching their way through all the dead leaves. Was it Joel checking I was all right? Or had my parents come looking for me? No, they hadn't a clue where I was, unless Joel had told them. Of course it could be Joel and my parents, all searching for me together.

But somehow I didn't think it was. It was someone else. I tried to move faster. But the quicker I ran, the sicker I felt. Then quite suddenly I tripped over something – couldn't see what it was – and went sprawling onto the ground.

A bird rose into the air with a sharp, warning cry. It sounded quite near me too. I decided to swallow my pride, ring my parents and tell them I was lost in the woods. I mean, how pathetic is that? I sounded about three. But I was ill and could hardly walk and I felt something edging closer to me. Something that filled me with fear, even if I didn't know who or what it was.

I needed reinforcements urgently.

So I fumbled about in my pocket for my mobile. Where was it? I was still searching for it when I heard the whisper of a wing right above my head. It must be a very inquisitive bird, I thought, come to see this strange creature lying on the ground.

But then I felt something touch my neck. It didn't feel like teeth or anything though. No, it was like being suddenly hit by a dart.

A poison dart.

Something started burning into my neck, while everything around me began slipping away. It was as if a black tide of sleep was rushing up my body. 'Help . . .' I managed to cry out. 'Help.'

The black tide was speeding up my chest towards my neck now. Then, just as it was clutching at my throat, I saw someone: I could hardly make them out at all – it was just the startling red eyes I noticed and a horrible sour smell. Then I must have passed out. So the next thing I knew, a torch was beamed right into my face. Blearily I made out someone – their eyes wide with horror. It was Tallulah.

I gaped at her, unsure if this was a dream or if she really was there. 'Get help,' I gasped. 'Been att . . . attacked.' After this dazzling piece of conversation, the black tide rolled right over me again and I passed out.

The next thing I actually remember is sitting up in bed, surrounded by my parents and the doctor.

'Well,' said the doctor, 'you've had quite a night, haven't you?'

'We won't be cross,' said Mum. 'But you've been eating garlic, haven't you?'

I nodded gravely.

'Oh, Marcus,' she cried. 'Eating garlic won't stop you being a half-vampire.'

'I never thought it would,' I said. 'I ate the garlic by accident.'

Three disbelieving faces stared down at me.

'No, honestly, I was just munching a pizza when I started to feel very ill. Then

I found out I'd eaten a garlic sausage.'

Mum let out a low moan. 'Oh, my poor boy.'

'Garlic is bad for vampires – and half-vampires – isn't it?' I said.

'You know it is,' said Dad.

'Well, you never actually told me,' I said.

'Of course we did,' said Dad. 'It's in the manual – to be sure and warn you.'

'Dad, you didn't,' I hissed.

Guilt jumped into my parents' faces. They stared at each other. 'I was sure we said something,' said Mum.

'Oh, well,' interrupted the doctor, 'there's so much information to impart at this time it's not surprising details get omitted. The thing about garlic, young man, is that half-vampires are highly allergic to it. And we always have a bad reaction. I expect you felt very sick afterwards.'

'I certainly did.'

'And all your energy seemed to have drained away and you had difficulty in concentrating,' went on the doctor. 'Sometimes it even gives us little hallucinations.'

I sat up in bed. 'Say more, Doc.'

'Oh well, it gets you imagining all sorts

of things. Is that what happened to you?'

I nodded. 'Scared myself, like you wouldn't believe.'

'All courtesy of the garlic you'd consumed,' said the doctor.

So all that stuff about me being attacked by a strange dart and then seeing those piercing red eyes had just been my garlic-fuelled imagination. I let out a huge sigh of relief.

And another one.

Mum was looking at me all anxiously again. 'Are you all right?'

'Never better, Mum. Well, no, that's not true of course, but tons better than I was . . . How exactly did I get here?'

'You were very foolish last night, running off without a word to your father or me,' said Mum.

'Have you any idea how worried we were when we found you'd gone?' said Dad.

'I'd hang my head in shame,' I said, 'if I could move it.'

'When we found you'd gone,' Mum went on, 'we guessed you'd disobeyed us and gone to the Monsters in School meeting. But we

123

didn't know where the meeting was. Then Joel turned up, wanting to check if you'd got home safely. When he told us you'd been taken ill, we were frantic with worry. We were searching in the woods when this girl came flying up to us.'

'Tallulah,' I murmured.

'That's right,' said Mum.

So I hadn't dreamed that part – Tallulah really had found me.

'She was most concerned about you too. Well, she showed us where you were and then your father and I carried you off to the car. We offered to drive her home but she said something about the woods being her real home and tore off again.'

'That sounds like Tallulah,' I muttered.

'Now, I hope lessons have been learned, you young blighter,' said the doctor. 'Notably, when your parents give you instructions, it's for a very good reason. You'll feel unwell for a few more hours yet – but no real harm done, provided you listen to me now. I want you to stay in bed for the rest of tomorrow – and keep this room quite dark too. Is that clear?'

'Totally,' I said.

'Ah well, I suppose we all have to try garlic once,' said the doctor. 'We rarely return to it a second time.' Then he turned his tiny left hand into a fist and shook it at me in mock anger. 'The next time I see you, Ved, I want you to have changed over successfully into a half-vampire. Is that clear?'

'I'll do my best.'

Right then I was so relieved to be home and safe that I'd have agreed to anything.

11.30 a.m.

This might sound like a really stupid question – but have you ever lost your reflection? Well, I have.

I'd just had a little breakfast when I noticed how itchy my neck felt. So I tumbled out of bed to check out what was happening.

I peeked into the mirror, only to discover I wasn't there.

I'd completely vanished.

I mean, I was there just as I'm here now. But somehow my reflection wasn't.

11.34 a.m.

Just had a second look in the mirror, and still

125

no sign of me, which is kind of worrying, actually. The undead don't cast any reflections either, do they? This thought doesn't exactly cheer me up. But I'm not panicking (much) as there's got to be a perfectly rational explanation for all this. Maybe it's just a reaction to eating garlic. Yeah, that could be it, couldn't it?

11.36 a.m.

I'm now wondering how long my reflection will stay away. You do get sort of used to having it around, don't you?

12.05 a.m.

I just casually mentioned to my mum that I didn't appear to have a reflection right now, hoping she'd say something highly reassuring like, 'Oh, those things are always going missing.' But instead she gave a little shriek and jumped right up into the air, which wasn't reassuring at all.

Then I told her about my neck being itchy. She looked even more alarmed (if that was possible) and asked if she could have a look at it.

'Yeah sure, feel free,' I said, but my heart was racing.

Then Mum gave a sharp gasp and said, in a very shocked voice, 'Your vampire jab.'

'What about it?'

'It looks different: bigger somehow and much redder, as if' – she said the next few words very slowly – 'you had a second bite there. But you weren't attacked last night, were you?'

'Yes and no,' I said. 'I mean, I do remember something flying towards me and biting my neck.' Mum gave another gasp. 'And I thought I saw someone with red eyes too, but then I figured it was just one of those hallucinations the doc mentioned. And I'd only imagined it all.'

Mum sat down on the bed. 'Tell me exactly what happened last night.'

So I did and she got more and more agitated. In the end, she shook her head at me and moaned, 'Oh, my poor Ved, if only you'd stayed in last night. If only.' And she looked as if she was about to burst into tears. This was not good.

'Er, Mum, do you think I really was attacked last night?'

'Yes,' she half whispered.

'By what?'

She immediately looked away.

'Mum, do you know what it was?'

'I think I do, yes,' said Mum, in a voice so quiet I could hardly hear her.

'So what was it?' I asked.

She looked away again.

'I don't want to appear nosy, but I would like to know,' I said.

Mum got up and went to the door.

'Oh no, don't run away, please . . . tell me.'

'I will, but I want to tell you properly,' said Mum. 'That's why I must call your father. He'll explain what's happened much better than me. And we'll need the doctor as well. I'll be back soon – so don't worry.'

Don't worry! My reflection had gone AWOL and I'd been attacked by something that's so terrible Mum couldn't talk about it on her own.

I'll tell you something, blog. I'd rather be a werewolf than a half-vampire any day. Actually, when it's not a full moon, werewolves have it dead easy. And anyway, turning a bit hairy and going on a rampage every now and again would be nothing compared to what I'm going through. It's just one sensationally awful thing after another, isn't it?

And right now I'm wondering just what my parents are going to tell me next.

CHAPTER ELEVEN

Friday 19 October
2.45 p.m.

Normally when your local doc pops in, he informs you that you're suffering from mumps or measles, or a nasty attack of skiving. This afternoon, it was totally different and the doctor told me . . . well I'm still reeling, if you really want to know.

Mum and Dad had been waiting so anxiously for him to arrive, continually peering out of the window, not wanting to say anything until he'd examined me. And when the doc's car finally pulled up, Dad just tore down the stairs.

But the doctor strolled in, smiling as usual.

'Well, here we are again,' he said breezily.

'We sure are,' I replied.

He got out a sort of two-way mirror and peered through it. Then he frowned.

'You can't see me either, can you?' I said.

'No, I'm afraid I can't,' he replied, looking up at Mum and Dad, who were clustered round us. 'And I don't like cases like this,' he said. 'To steal someone's reflection seems such a colossal cheek. And we half-vampires, contrary to popular myth, like to keep our reflections close by.'

'Someone has stolen it then,' I said.

'I'm afraid they have, yes,' said the doctor.

'Who?' I asked.

The doctor looked up at Mum and Dad as if to ask permission to say something serious. Dad nodded gravely. 'Well, it's time I told you a few facts, Ved,' said the doctor. 'Your parents have tried to spare you this – as they didn't want to worry you unnecessarily.'

'We hoped you'd never have to know,' said Mum quickly.

'Look, don't worry about me, I'm brave. Hey, what am I saying? The Tooth Fairy gave me nightmares.'

'We don't want to give you any more night-mares,' said Dr Jasper smoothly. 'Now, did you know we half-vampires have only been around for about three hundred and fifty years?'

'So we're just babies really,' I muttered.

'But vampires have walked this earth for thousands of years.'

I gave a little gulp. 'You're talking real vampires now.'

'Oh yes, but don't believe everything you've read about them. Just as wolves – despite the myths – rarely attack humans, the same is true of vampires. They are much more likely to gain their supply of blood from cows or sheep. How often have you read about such animals being attacked by a mystery predator? That's when you see vampires at work. In fact, vampires don't even like human blood very much.'

'But all the stories—' I began.

He chuckled. 'All highly inaccurate. In reality, human blood doesn't suit vampires at all. To them, it tastes like very sour milk. But I'm afraid there's one exception.' He paused for a moment. 'Half-vampires, when they are going through their changeover – now, their blood is very attractive to vampires indeed.'

'Well, that news has really cheered me up,' I said, as a shudder ran through me.

The doc continued. 'And vampires can easily pick up the scent of half-vampires during their changeover . . . and then, well, they can't help gravitating towards you.'

'That's why,' burst out Mum, 'we wanted you to change over quickly. Some children turn into half-vampires really swiftly and are never bothered after that.'

'Because,' said Dr Jasper, 'half-vampires' blood is as unappetizing to a vampire as human blood. It is only in the phase that you are in now that you are a prime target.'

'This is a lot to take in, isn't it?' said Dad. 'Are you all right?'

'Oh yeah, I've swallowed my tongue with shock,' I said, 'but otherwise I'm groovy. So it was a vampire who attacked me last night?'

Both Mum and Dad turned away as if they couldn't bear to answer. 'Yes, Ved, I'm afraid it was,' said Dr Jasper at last. 'The vampire had been tracking you for a while.'

So when I thought someone was close by last night it wasn't just me imagining stuff. My friendly local vampire really was hovering nearby, just waiting for the right moment to strike.

The doctor went on, 'All vampires can transform themselves into bats. That much of the legend is true. Well, half-vampires can too, actually. And vampires often prefer to strike first in the form of a bat.'

'So when I felt that dart on my neck . . .' I began.

Dr Jasper looked at my parents as if to say – You'd better tell him the next bit.

And then Dad said briskly, 'Yes, it really was the bat, Marcus. One tiny bite would be enough to knock you out. Then the vampire assumes its normal form.'

I thought again of those huge, red eyes which I'd just glimpsed for a second. 'But why didn't it just kill me? Not that I'm complaining or anything.'

Dr Jasper smiled at me and my parents. 'Again you are allowing yourself to be too influenced by the wild excesses of the cinema. Vampires won't kill you but they will take away something of you, such as your strength and—'

'Your reflection,' I interrupted. 'And will that vampire be back for me again?'

The doctor sighed. 'That is the most distressing part. I'm afraid it is close by – even now waiting for its moment to strike once more. And if it does it will take even more of you.'

'And I can't spare a single molecule. So how do we fight it?'

'The vampire's power is much greater than ours,' said the doctor apologetically.

'So whichever way you look at it, us half-vampires are pretty pathetic really,' I said.

'Now now,' said Dr Jasper. 'It is this bad attitude which has got you into all this trouble. The moment you turn into a half-vampire you will instantly cease to be of any interest to our local vampire.'

'But until then it could attack me at any time?' I asked.

'Unlikely in the day. Vampires are usually perfectly respectable people, unsuspected by anyone. By the way, all the old stories about vampires turning into dust by day are nonsense. Vampires are merely wary of the sun and usually very well wrapped up if they have to go out in it. One more fact: your attacker is almost certainly someone you have already met.'

'Like a headmaster,' I said at once.

'Well, it could be, I suppose,' said the doctor. He went on, 'Vampires have this strange code of etiquette: they only like to feed off someone they have met before. Ideally they will be invited into their house. But a vampire might just be someone who stops to talk to you in the street. Some vampires – especially very hungry ones – will count that as making your acquaintance. But they are very careful about breaking their cover. Also, they are far more powerful when it gets dark, and if the vampire strikes again, it will almost certainly be at night. So no more nocturnal adventures, young man. Until you change over to a half-vampire you are "in season" and in grave danger.'

'We'll never let you out of our sight again,' said Mum.

I tried hard to look grateful, but actually, I thought, never being out of my parents' sight was nearly as bad as being attacked by a vampire.

'And you must stay in bed until your reflection comes back fully,' said the doctor. 'It will return – this time. The first sign of this is you will start to become very thirsty and want to drink gallons of water.' He got up. 'And don't be down-hearted, as I've a piece of good news for you.'

'What's that?' I ask.

'I think your cravings have stopped,' he said.

'Perhaps they took off with my reflection,' I replied.

4.30 p.m.

Still missing: one reflection of a cheeky-looking boy with thick black hair and a big red bite on his neck. If found, please return to owner as soon as possible.

4.45 p.m.

A text from Joel asking how I am. Wouldn't he get the shock of his life if I answered that question honestly? He also said that Tallulah has been asking about me and sent her regards. Her regards . . . that's what bank managers send you.

But here's a very odd thing: it was Tallulah who found me and went speeding off to get help, but she can't have said one word about this to Joel. Or surely he'd have mentioned it. Why wouldn't she tell him?

And seeing the state I was in last night, would it have killed her to send me a text message herself, just to check I'm still alive?

And yes, I know I should be grateful to Tallulah for finding my parents and all that stuff. And I am. But I'm also— Oh, I don't know why I'm rabbiting on about her. I do have a few other things to worry about right now. Like a vampire who at the moment is probably lurking outside my house craving some more of my high-powered blood.

That's a nice, cheerful thought, blog, isn't it?

4.55 p.m.

Do you know what I'd like more than any-thing else right now? Not to be a millionaire or a world-class footballer. Not even to be a professional chocolate-taster. I just want to go back to being a normal human being again. If I could do that, I wouldn't ever ask for anything else.

But it's the one thing I can never do. No, I either stay like this, watching out all the time for any vampires passing who might be stalking me (and vampires can smell me hundreds of miles away apparently, I knew I was using the wrong deodorant!) or I change over into a half-vampire. That's it; there aren't any other choices for me.

And I'll always have this huge, stinking secret right in the middle of my life. A secret which I can never escape from. My life is tilted towards deeply weird for good.

Just writing that last sentence has made me feel a whole lot worse. So I'll stop now.

6.30 p.m.

I've reached a decision. I'm going to give it a shot, and try my hardest to become a half-vampire.

Did the news that there's a vampire hanging about with my name on its fangs affect my decision at all? Me? I laugh in

the face of danger – then run like mad.
So, yes!
Yes! Yes!

6.50 p.m.

My parents come into my bedroom, both looking truly awful. I know I've given them a
mountain of stress and do have a small pang
of guilt about that (even though it was their
rubbish genetics which has landed me in all
this) but I tell them of my decision.

Instantly they look so happy and relieved.
'You won't regret this,' says Dad. Then he
rather shyly digs out of my wardrobe one
very neglected vampire cape. Looking at it
again, I can see it's pretty impressive in
its bizarre way. Dad places it around my
shoulders, but I put it on properly. This
makes my parents whoop and cheer. They're
so easily pleased.

Then I announce, 'I am a half-vampire.'
They clap their hands in ecstasy.

'Now I know for certain,' says Dad, 'you
will be a half-vampire very soon. And make
us very proud of you.'

'Not that we aren't already,' lied Mum.

9.50 p.m.

For the first time in ages, I shan't say 'I am not a half-vampire' before I go to sleep, because what's the point? I'm in my parents' world of vampires and half-vampires. And nothing I can do will stop that.

But here's what's bothering me: what if for some reason I can't cross over into being a half-vampire, or what if I'm not cut out to be one?

Does that mean I'm stuck like this for ever?

10.45 p.m.

I'm more and more certain I know who the vampire is: it's Townley. Well, he's angry enough to be one – and he's got absolutely no sense of humour. I can just picture him slurping blood too. And he's always going on about how he's watching me. I bet every time I walk past him he takes a deep appreciative sniff, as the scent of my half-vampire blood floats into his nostrils. Oh, it'd be so great if it was him. I'd love to expose him – the Vampire Headmaster. Any other suspects?

Well, I remember a car pulling up the

other day after school and a man in very thick glasses asking me for directions. He was very chatty too. Could that have been the vampire introducing himself to me?

No, it's Townley. Got to be.

11.05 p.m.
My parents are checking on me – yet again. Yeah, it's good of them to be so bothered but it also reminds me that the vampire is watching, waiting out there. Then Dad whispers that he has a great surprise for me tomorrow.

Saturday 20 October
9.45 a.m.

I've just found out what the surprise is. And it's not great at all. In fact, it's absolutely terrible.

CHAPTER TWELVE

**Saturday 20 October
9.55 a.m.**

Next to being chased by a vampire, what's the very worst thing that could happen to me?

That's right, having Cousin Karl slither back into my world. And get this: he is to be my very own bodyguard and coach. So he isn't just dropping by for a visit. No, he'll be with me practically night and day – until I change over. So if I don't ever change over, does that mean I'll never be free of him? My parents actually think I'll be pleased by this news.

'But you got on so well,' said Mum.

'No, we didn't,' I answered.

'But he's very keen,' went on Mum. 'He rang up especially to hear how you're getting on and he really thinks he can help.'

'Cancel him,' I cried. 'I'm begging you.'

'But he's on his way,' said Mum. 'We've even worked out where he can stay: up in the attic. He'll be very comfortable there.'

11.15 a.m.

Hell's teeth, he's here.

He came blustering into my bedroom, looking even more pleased with himself than usual (if that's possible). Then he said, rubbing his hands together, 'You're in the deepest danger of your whole life – and you haven't got any reflection. Now, what on earth is that like? I couldn't imagine looking into a mirror and not seeing myself there.'

'It's great actually,' I said, 'because now I never have to worry what I look like.'

'Well, you do,' said Karl, 'because we can all still see you . . .'

'Oh no,' I said. 'I never realized that. So you can see me now?'

Karl looked at me for a moment. 'I've come here to help you, Ved, with all your tons of problems. So what would you like me to do first?'

'Disappear?' I said hopefully.

'It's great you can make jokes – even at a time like this.'

'That wasn't a joke,' I murmured.

'Now, how about if we get you thinking vampire by practising some roars. I'll do one first,' he added eagerly.

He did, and of course it was brilliant. Yawn! Yawn!

'Now try and copy me,' he continued.

So I did and it was just pitiful. Nowhere near as good as that roar I did at school. The one Tallulah overheard.

'I think you're putting me off,' I said.

'I can see that,' he said. 'You're worried you can't roar as well as me. And you probably can't. But don't worry, you can still be a perfectly good roarer – if not a world-class one. Shall I go away?'

'Oh, yes please.'

'How far should I go?' he asked.

'Back home.'

'Always the joker. Look, I'll just stand outside the door.'

He listened to my next attempt and then oiled back in, looking very stern. 'Ved, you can't just luck into being a half-vampire, you know. You've got to at least try.'

The trouble was, I had been trying.

Karl let out a big sigh. 'You're feeling tense and frustrated, aren't you?'

'Yes, I am,' I admitted.

'And how long have you been feeling like this?'

'Since you arrived,' I said.

He rubbed his hands together – one of his many annoying habits. 'You're going to be my biggest challenge. But don't worry, I'll win in the end.'

I looked up. 'Will you?'

'Oh yes,' he said, oozing confidence as usual. 'I always win.'

CHAPTER THIRTEEN

Saturday 20 October
2.50 p.m.

I've just had a visitor.

Mum answered the door and called up, 'A friend to see you, Marcus.'

'Send Joel up,' I said, just assuming it would be him.

'It's Tallulah actually,' said Mum, sounding a bit excited. And my heart gave a huge thump too. This surprised me.

'Oh, well send her up,' I said, trying to sound as casual as I could.

Tallulah chatted to Mum for a few more seconds and next I heard her walk quickly up the stairs. My heart gave another thump.

And then Karl had to stick his nose in. I heard him saying to Tallulah at the top of the stairs, 'You can only stay a few minutes.'

'Rubbish,' I yelled. 'You can stay as long as you like. Bring a sleeping bag if you want.'

Tallulah strolled into my room with Karl right behind her as if he were my butler, bodyguard and dad, all rolled into one.

'So how are you?' she asked.

Before I could reply Karl declared, 'He's not at all well – got a virus.'

Seeing a look of alarm cross Tallulah's face, I cut in, 'But it's only a tiny, little virus – and not infectious in the slightest. By the way, that guy lurking beside you is a very, very distant relation, but I won't bother introducing you, as he's just leaving.'

Even Karl took the hint. 'I'll be outside if you need me,' he said.

'Why on earth should we need you?' I replied.

'Well,' said Karl to Tallulah, 'he's certainly perked up since you came in.' That guy couldn't be more embarrassing if he tried.

After he'd finally left I said, 'I apologize for

him. He keeps his brain in a jar. But we have to humour him as he's my eighth cousin twice removed or something. But why are we talking about him anyway? It's me you came to see, and who can blame you?'

'Shy and modest as ever,' Tallulah said. And we both sort of laughed and I sensed she was nearly as nervous as me. But the astonishing, and the truly incredible thing, was how pleased I was to see her.

'How long did the M.I.S. meeting go on for after I left?' I asked.

'Not long,' said Tallulah. 'No one could concentrate after . . .'

'I'm really sorry for messing up your meeting,' I said.

'No, it's all right,' she said. 'We've set up another one for tomorrow now. You'll miss that, but we'll probably have one during the week too so you should come to that.'

'Hey, you're being nice to me. Now I know I must be ill.'

'Well, I shan't be nice to you ever again. So enjoy this moment,' said Tallulah.

'By the way, thanks for—'

'I don't do thanks,' she snapped, 'because I

just go bright red and it's horrible.' She was reddening a bit as she said this.

I had a horrible feeling my face had burst into Technicolor too.

'I'll just say it was lucky you were close by,' I said.

'Yes, OK,' she said. Then she started circling round my room. Watching her made me feel slightly dizzy. But I was still awed that she was here visiting me. And shockingly happy about it as well.

'Just before you passed out,' she said, 'you mentioned something about being attacked.' She looked questioningly at me.

'I must have dreamed that,' I said, not feeling at all easy about lying to Tallulah. After all, she had rescued me. But there was no way I could tell her the truth. I was talking rubbish, as usual. I said quickly, 'In fact, I just tripped over in the mist.' Then I added, 'You didn't tell Joel or anyone else that you'd found me.'

'No,' she said, stopping her pacing suddenly. 'I thought you'd rather I kept that to myself.'

'I would actually,' I said, grinning at her.

'Not my finest hour, was it, getting lost in the woods and falling over and having to be rescued by my ickle mummy and daddy.'

'But you weren't yourself, Marcus,' she said. She was just so different from the grim, permanently scowling Tallulah I knew from school.

She came closer, leaned right over me in fact, her eyes shining with a strange light. And then something truly astonishing occurred. She kissed me.

Just a light kiss on my left cheek. But still, a girl had voluntarily kissed me – and looked as if she'd enjoyed herself too. I tell you, this was nearly as incredible as discovering I'm from a family of half-vampires.

'Wow,' I said, 'I wasn't expecting that.'

'Neither was I,' she replied, another great wave of colour rushing into her normally pale face.

We were really having a little moment there when bellowing across the room came: 'Tallulah, would you like a hot drink at all – tea or coffee or hot chocolate?'

Yes, Karl was back, only now he'd turned into a waiter.

'Er, no thanks,' said Tallulah.

He persisted. 'What about a cold drink? We've got—'

'No, I've got to go actually.' She seemed flustered and awkward now. Trust Karl to break the spell.

'Here's a great idea,' I said to Karl. 'Why don't you go away and have a hot drink *and* a cold drink?' But it was too late. Tallulah was already at the door.

'Look after yourself,' she said suddenly, not able to look at me directly. That kiss had obviously taken her by surprise and now she was clearly embarrassed by it.

'Well, call again, any time,' I cried. 'We never close.'

After she'd gone I was lying there glowing – that's the only word for it – until you-know-who had to strut in and spoil it all.

'Very odd,' he announced.

'What is?'

'That girl coming to see you. Felt wrong.'

I stared at him. 'What are you talking about?'

'This is not what you want to hear, and sorry to be the bearer of such tidings – but you're not her type.'

'How do you know?' I shouted.

'Got an eye for these things. So this was the girl who found you in the woods, was it?'

'Yes,' I snapped.

'Hmm, so what was she doing there?'

'Well, anyone can wander about in the woods. And I don't think she's very happy at home, so she wades about thinking up stories. But what's this got to do with anything anyway?'

'There's something suspicious about that girl,' said Karl. 'Mark my words.'

I glared at him. 'Did you go on a course to be so totally annoying – or does it just come naturally?'

'I know I'm telling you something you'd rather not hear,' said Karl in a slow, patronizing voice. 'So I will accept any insults you hurl at me.'

'Look,' I cried, getting really angry now. 'Apart from wanting to see how I am, what other possible reason could Tallulah have for visiting me?'

'I don't know yet,' said Karl. 'But I'm just saying, be very careful. That girl is up to something.'

4.55 p.m.

Some people are lower than a snake's bottom. And Karl is one of those. He couldn't let me think that a girl might like me a bit, so he plants all that garbage about Tallulah being up to something.

5.10 p.m.

Karl is a smarmy, oily, big-headed weasel, who I couldn't stand before, and now I positively hate.

5.20 p.m.

We are agreed that Tallulah came to see me for no other reason than she wanted to find out how I was.

Good, and thanks, blog, for clearing that up once and for all.

I don't know what I'd do without you.

CHAPTER FOURTEEN

Sunday 21 October
6.15 a.m.

Woke up gasping for water. My throat had never felt so dry. I tried to call out, but in the end I used the bell Karl had placed right by my bed. He'd been sleeping on a little chair outside my bedroom. He charged in with a jug of water, but tripped and managed to pour half of it all over me. I was so thirsty I just tried to lick up any water that had landed near my lips.

6.50 a.m.
Gulping water down now. Just can't drink enough. Mum and Dad, hovering anxiously,

say this is a good sign. It means I'm getting back to normal.

8.50 a.m.
Hey, my reflection is on its way back. Still a bit misty, but at least it's there. Funny how lost I felt without it.

9.15 a.m.
The doctor called. 'Yes, we've stopped the vampire infection this time,' he said proudly.

'What about if the vampire catches me again?' I croak.

'Oh, come come,' said the doctor. 'Put away such gloomy thoughts.'

'But it's close by, isn't it, waiting to strike once more?'

'The moment you change over into a half-vampire it will scuttle away into the darkness where it belongs. So come along now, Ved, just relax your mind and let your natural vampire side come through.'

9.50 a.m.
And I wanted to do this, I really did. I was sick of being in this kind of limbo. But I'd just

started relaxing my mind when Karl stalked in. 'I've made a list of things you must do.' And straight away he made my hackles rise.

'I'll make my own list, thanks,' I said.

Karl bristled. 'I do know what I'm talking about. I did change over into a half-vampire in forty-eight hours which, I still believe, is a record.'

'So what's it like being so colossally brilliant?' I asked.

'Sarcasm,' he muttered, 'is not helpful. Now, number one on my list is, you need to do some reading. That's dead easy, even for you.' He threw a pile of books and magazines on my bed. 'But the important thing is to get the half-vampire vibe.' Then he let out a loud howl.

'Hey, what did you do that for?' I asked.

'You've got to look after your howl, so practice is very important. I do forty howls a day.'

'I bet you're popular with the neighbours,' I quipped.

'Extremely popular, actually,' he said a bit huffily. 'Now, shall I move on to number two on my list?'

'No,' I said firmly.

'Bad attitude equals failure, good attitude means success. I'm going to leave that thought with you.'

'It's all right, you can take it with you.'

Karl made as if to leave and then came back. 'You didn't like what I said about that girl, Tallulah, did you?'

'I never gave it a second thought,' I said. Yeah, OK – a great big whopping lie. But I didn't want Karl to know he'd got to me.

'I'm completely right about her,' Karl said. 'You'll see.'

5.25 p.m.

I got up and was pottering around my bedroom when I saw Tallulah hovering right outside my house. I quickly brushed my hair, expecting her to ring on the doorbell any second. Only she never did. Instead, she just disappeared.

So why come all the way to my house and then scarper. What was the point of that?

5.35 p.m.

I've worked it out. She's obviously really

really missing me – and who can blame her?
– but is too shy to call in so soon after her last
visit.

5.38 p.m.
Just call me the love god.

5.42 p.m.
I've sent Tallulah a cheeky little text saying:
'Good luck with the meeting tonight, wish I
could come along, but I'm off school until
Wednesday.' I ended by saying it was great to
see her yesterday. I didn't put love or anything. But I wanted to say something more
than regards. So I wrote 'very best wishes'
with a tiny x beside it.

9.05 p.m.
She hasn't replied – I wasn't expecting her to,
actually. But anyway, she hasn't.

9.25 p.m.
Spent the day swotting up on vampires. Read
tons. And this evening I let out a vampire
howl which wasn't completely terrible. Mum
and Dad were getting quite excited.

Mum said, 'Tomorrow morning we want to see you sporting a yellow fang.' That'd mean I'd crossed over, of course. And I wanted to see it too. That's why I've been chanting 'I'm a half-vampire' all day.

I'm even trying to get used to my half-vampire name. I suppose there are worse names than Ved. I just haven't thought of any yet.

11.15 p.m.

Dad's crept in again, just to check the vampire hasn't somehow slipped into the house and attacked me.

Now, I don't ever want to meet that vampire again. But I'd so love to know who it is. Especially as it's someone I actually knew. He or she could be any age too. So it might even be a person in my class. No, it's Mr 'I shall be watching you closely' Townley. He's got to be the number one suspect. It's a good job I'm not going to school for a few days, then. He won't be able to get at me.

11.35 p.m.

Now Mum's been sneaking a look at me.

Wouldn't it be great if this is the last night
we'll have to worry about a vampire visitor?

And tomorrow I might wake up sprouting
one yellow fang.

CHAPTER FIFTEEN

Monday 22 October
6.45 a.m.

No fang!

7.05 a.m.
Mum and Dad rush in, all hopeful. They can't believe I'm still fangless. They don't say anything but Mum draws back my curtains with smouldering disappointment.

7.08 a.m.
I feel bad for them, blog.

I feel bad for me.

It's no fun hovering like this between two identities. I really don't know what I am at

162

the moment. And I could stay like this for days, if not months, even years.

9.15 a.m.

Karl brings in still more vampire books for me to read. Feel as if I'm revising for an exam I'll never pass.

10.45 a.m.

Karl hardly speaks to me today. This is great news – only I sense even he has given up on me now.

2.00 p.m.

I come downstairs, after which I'm out of breath. My energy is returning very slowly. Dad is home all day today. He won't say why. But his face is riddled with anxiety.

2.50 p.m.

My parents are talking together in hushed whispers. I crawl out towards the kitchen to try and catch what they're saying because it's bound to be about me. But they hear me and quickly change the subject. Later they start whispering again, this time with

Karl. Something is definitely going on.

4.25 p.m.

Joel has just called round.

'Now, first of all,' he announced, 'I want you to breathe all over me and cough right in my face too. I'm just in the mood for a nice, fat virus as I really fancy a week off school, lolling at home. In fact, I can't think of anything better.'

'You wouldn't like this virus,' I said.

'Yes, I would. So come on, don't be stingy, share it around.'

'Actually it's not a very infectious virus,' I said.

He exclaimed indignantly: 'What, you're a total let-down! And is it true you caught it from that pizza at the meeting?'

'No, it isn't,' I said at once.

'Oh, I thought your slice of pizza was just crawling with bugs and germs. And I was wondering how you managed to get so lucky.' Joel lowered his voice. 'So where is he then? This mad cousin Tallulah was telling me about.'

'Oh, I've hardly seen him today,' I said.

'Shame, because I love loonies – well, I'm friends with you, aren't I?' I made as if to hit him and then asked about last night's M.I.S. meeting.

'But it was cancelled at the last minute,' he said.

'Why?' I asked.

Joel shrugged. 'Tallulah never gave a reason, just said it was postponed until Wednesday night. So do you think you'll be able to make that one?'

'Yeah, I should think so,' I said.

'Well then, I've got this for you. It's top secret, so I had strict instructions not to open it. This contains your next challenge. And although I was very tempted, I haven't even had a peek, can you believe that?'

He handed me an envelope with FOR THE ATTENTION OF MARCUS HOWLETT written across it.

'You're supposed to open it after I've gone, but we can ignore that bit, can't we?'

'Definitely,' I said, ripping open the envelope, sort of chuffed that Tallulah had thought up this new challenge – at least that

165

proved she'd been thinking about me – and who can blame her?

Then I stared at the message, totally stunned by what it said. For it wasn't a challenge at all. Instead, she'd written in block capitals:

MARCUS, IT IS VITAL I SEE YOU TONIGHT. MEET ME AT MONSTERS' MEETING PLACE AT SEVEN O'CLOCK. IT IS VERY URGENT. TELL NO ONE ABOUT THIS MESSAGE. COME ALONE. TALLULAH.

'So what does it say then?' asked Joel.

And I really wanted to tell him. For it was such an extraordinary message. Why would Tallulah want to see me so urgently? What possible reason could she have? I badly needed to discuss this with someone, and Joel was the obvious choice.

But she'd underlined TELL NO ONE. So I said: 'Oh, she's just saying she wants me to prepare properly for the meeting next time or I'll be chucked out.'

'That's harsh,' said Joel at once. 'It wasn't

your fault the friendly virus struck when it did.' He lowered his voice. 'I know M.I.S. is her idea, and a brilliant one. But she's majorly bossy, isn't she?'

I could agree there: summoning me to the meeting place tonight seemed incredibly bossy. Only her message didn't quite sound like that. No, it was more worried and scared and practically begging, rather than commanding me to turn up. But why? Why?

'You're looking dead worried,' said Joel suddenly.

'No, not me,' I said airily.

'Yes, you are, I can tell. But don't let her get to you. I'll have a think about a horror story and ring you up with it; and if the Bride of Dracula doesn't like that, we'll form our own alternative M.I.S. How about that?'

And then Mum, Dad and Karl piled in. Joel was introduced to Karl and then Dad said, 'Hate to break things up, but we'd really like to have a little word with Marcus.'

'That's OK,' said Joel. 'If I'd known Marcus's bug wasn't infectious I wouldn't have bothered visiting him anyway.' Then he winked at me and added, half under his breath, 'And don't worry about this new challenge, I'll be in contact.'

This deputation of my parents and Karl now faced me.

'Just to let you know,' said Mum a bit too brightly, 'that your dad and I are popping up to London tonight.'

'Why are you doing that?' I demanded at once.

A slight pause before Dad said, 'We want to get some advice.'

'About me?' I asked.

'Yes,' said Dad. 'Karl has given us the address of a consultant.'

'A half-vampire consultant?' I said.

'That's right,' said Dad. 'The country's leading one. So we've done well getting an appointment with him. And then we're hoping he will come and see you.'

'You make me feel a right freak.'

'You're not exactly a freak,' began Karl.

'You're not a freak at all,' said Mum firmly. 'But your father and I just want to do the best for you. We shouldn't be long, but while we're away Karl will be in charge; all right?'

5.10 p.m.

With Mum and Dad out tonight, that leaves only Karl to sneak past when I go and meet Tallulah. Oh yeah, I'm definitely going. Well, I've got to know what this is all about.

6.30 p.m.

Mum and Dad have left. But Karl will probably turn into a half-human clamp. How can I possibly break away from him?

6.41 p.m.

The good news, the very, very good news – is that Karl has gone up to the attic to practise his howling. He likes to do forty every evening. He says he'll be down soon to question me about all the vampire stories I've been reading today. But right now he's left me on my own.

6.50 p.m.

You have to slam our front door shut and Karl might just hear that. So instead, I open the sitting-room window, which leads directly to the front garden. I scramble out and now I'm on my way to the woods.

Unfortunately, I'm moving at the pace of an arthritic snail.

7.00 p.m.

I've reached the woods at last. And it's suddenly hit me what a mad thing I'm doing. I'm returning at night to the very place the vampire attacked me last time. Only now I've got the energy level of a hundred-and-twenty year-old.

7.04 p.m.

Just had the strangest feeling that I'm being watched once more. I stumble forward as quickly as I can. Will I be calling Tallulah for help again? It was just so lucky she was in the woods before.

7.05 p.m.

A mad thought pops into my head, so insane I feel bad even writing it down. But here it is. What if it wasn't luck Tallulah popped up before? What if she'd been trailing me, waiting for the right moment to strike? And then after she'd had her fill of my blood she turned up again and cleverly pretended to rescue me?

And the secret message she sent me tonight is just a trap to get me into the woods again so she can have a blood top-up. I hastily swat such a thought away.

Tallulah, a vampire? Impossible.

7.15 p.m.

The cricket pavilion is just ahead. I'm not very late. And I'm sure Tallulah will have waited for me – now I'll find out what this urgent summons is all about.

CHAPTER SIXTEEN

Monday 22 October
7.55 p.m.

I was only about a quarter of an hour late when I arrived at the Monsters in School meeting place. It looked very different this time, of course. No candlelight, no figures in masks: just Tallulah and me in a dark, musty-smelling room.

She rushed over to me. 'How are you feeling, Marcus?' Her voice was surprisingly gentle and she was smiling at me in a way— Well, let's say girls don't normally smile at me like that. I wondered suddenly if we'd kiss again tonight.

'I'm feeling as good as new – if not better,' I said confidently.

We grinned at each other and I wondered how I could ever have thought she was a vampire. Insane or what? It must have been Karl's influence, poisoning my mind. Tallulah went on grinning at me – I'd never seen her so gentle and nice – and I was putting it all down to my awesome magnetism, when she said softly, 'Marcus, I know.'

'Good,' I said encouragingly. Then I added, 'Know what?'

'I know your secret,' she said, just a trifle impatiently.

'What secret is that then?' I asked.

'I know you didn't fall over in the woods that night – you were attacked.' My heart beat even faster. 'And, Marcus, I know you were attacked by a vampire because that night in the woods when I found you, I saw the bite mark on your neck.'

My face tingled. Then I tried to laugh.

'No, don't you laugh at me,' said Tallulah firmly. 'I'm an expert on monsters. And when I shone the torch I saw the mark of the vampire high up on the left side of your neck. Vampires always attack you on the left side and they have a favourite spot too, exactly where you were attacked.'

My throat felt very tight now. 'Look, Tallulah—' I croaked.

'Please don't lie,' she snapped. 'This means too much to me.'

'OK,' I croaked.

'And afterwards I did wonder if somehow I'd imagined it. That's why I had to check, and I did. That night at your house when I leaned over to kiss you.'

My whole body froze. 'So that's why you kissed me, is it?'

'Oh yes,' she said, without a particle of guilt. 'And I saw it again – the mark of a vampire just on the left side . . .'

But I'd stopped listening to her. Instead, I was too busy reflecting on how my life totally and completely stinks.

I mean, I've grown fangs, had cravings for blood and been attacked by a vampire – to name just a few of the past few weeks' highlights. But I could cope with all that – and more – because one night a girl, who for some mad reason I like, had turned up at my house and kissed me.

That made up for everything else. Only

now, even that's been snatched away from me.

Tallulah was staring at me, all flushed and excited, while I said in a cool, clipped voice, 'So, just for the record, when you came to see me it was purely so you could check out your theory – your insane theory – that I'd been attacked by a vampire?'

'I had to know, Marcus. It was all I could think about.'

'Well, to make your day I will say yes, I *was* attacked by a vampire.'

She gave a thrilled gasp.

'And then I was rescued by a kindly unicorn. That's how I got home. It let me ride on its back. It was remarkably comfortable actually, and it could fly, which was so handy. Then who was waiting for me when I got home? Only Father Christmas. A bit early, but he thought I needed cheering up—'

'Stop!' she shouted at me. 'Why are you saying all this rubbish?'

'Because I thought that's what you wanted,' I said. 'I haven't told you Aladdin popped in too. He was just back from a date with Cinderella and—'

'Shut up, you're not funny,' she said.

'At least I'm not mad, going round kissing boys because you think they've been attacked by a . . . a totally fictional creature.'

'I know what I saw on your neck,' she cried.

'What you saw on my neck was a jab which I had recently.'

'No, it wasn't,' she cried, shaking her head fervently.

'You'd like me to have been attacked by a vampire, wouldn't you?'

And do you know, she actually hesitated.

'In fact, it'd have made your day,' I half yelled.

'No, of course I didn't want you to be hurt,' she said finally.

'Sorry, don't believe you,' I said. 'But then you never have time for anyone, do you?'

'That's not true.'

'Yes, it is. Well, you hate all your family for a start. And there's not a girl in the whole school who can even bear to talk to you. In fact, you haven't got one single friend.'

'Yes, I have.'

'Who?'

'Oh, just shut up!' she suddenly shouted at me.

'No, the only people you like,' I shouted back, 'are totally made-up monsters. You're not bothered about real people, like me.'

'But I am. That's why I had to warn you. Once vampires get a taste for your blood, they often return for more.'

'Which story did you read that in?' I asked.

'Marcus, I am certain you've been attacked by a vampire – and are now in great danger. And I'm trained to know all about vampires.'

'Trained,' I muttered disbelievingly. 'Who trained you then?'

'Actually, I trained myself.'

I started to laugh.

'No, don't laugh, I've done months and months of research on this—'

'No, you've just read loads of stupid stories.'

'Listen to me,' she cried. 'You are in grave danger.'

Well, she was on the money there but I still snapped, 'I'd rather be attacked by a band of blood-crazed vampires than spend another second with you. And don't ever try kissing me again.' Then I stomped off.

I thought she'd yell something rude after me for that, but instead she called, 'Marcus, please listen to me. You've definitely been attacked by a vampire and it will return. I'm right about this. So be very careful when you're going through the woods, won't you?'

'Your concern makes me want to heave,' I yelled back.

But I hurried back through the woods as fast as I could. I'd be such an easy target for a vampire now as my body just ached with tension and tiredness. No doubt Karl would really tell me off when I got back. Well, I suppose I deserved it. It was insane to go wandering off when I was still 'in season', as the doctor put it.

I just had to keep moving. And finally I was out of those eerily still woods. I breathed a sigh of relief. I was bitterly disappointed though by what had happened. I'd really thought . . . but I've wasted too much time thinking about Tallulah.

I quickly scrambled back inside the house through the still-open window, the curtains flapping like sails. Immediately I heard Karl calling me. I sped towards him in the hallway. 'Ah, there you are,' he said. 'Hope you've been studying those vampire books I gave you,' he said.

'Oh, yes,' I lied.

So Karl hadn't even noticed I'd slipped out. That was a piece of luck. His hair was a bit dishevelled, as if he'd just woken up. I'd suspected for a while that he took afternoon naps.

'You still look very groggy,' he said.

'Thanks so much for that.'

'And I don't want you slipping out to meet that Tallulah,' said Karl with a little smile. Well, he was just a bit late on this one. So I smiled grimly as he locked the front door and pocketed the key.

'Now I shall prepare my special tonic for you,' said Karl, striding towards the kitchen. 'This will sort you out.'

I didn't argue. I was too tired, to be honest – and very relieved to be home and safe.

9.45 p.m.

Only I wasn't safe at all.

CHAPTER SEVENTEEN

Monday 22 October
9.46 p.m.

Oh yeah, the vampire has returned.

What a night this has been.

It started – and already that seems light centuries away – with Karl babbling on in the kitchen about this wonderful tonic he was making for me and how it'd give me so much energy . . . when the phone in the hall rang. We don't get very many calls on the land line now and I just assumed it was someone selling something or a wrong number. But instead, a voice said quite excitedly, 'Oh hello, is that Marcus?'

'I claim that honour – so who's this?'

'I don't expect you recognize my voice, after all this time.'

'You're right, I don't.'

'But we heard from a friend of a friend that you've been trying to contact us.' He lowered his voice here. 'You're going through something I know all about.'

'Well, that's great, but who exactly are you?'

He laughed. 'Oh yeah, sorry – it's your cousin Karl.'

I nearly dropped the phone with shock.

'Wh . . . aat?'

'Yeah, I think the last time we met was at Cousin Fred's wedding, but you probably don't remember that.' Still stunned, I just mumbled something.

'And my parents and I have been in America these past months, but we're back earlier than we expected. So I just wondered how it was all going . . .'

'Well . . .' I began.

'I know you don't want to say very much on the phone – very wise. But you haven't crossed over yet?'

'No, there have been a few little problems,' I said.

'Oh, I know all about that,' he said and laughed just as the kitchen door opened and there was – Karl.

Trust me, moments don't get much weirder than that. Talking to my cousin Karl on the phone, while by the kitchen door stood another cousin Karl. Only this one was clutching something too: a small glass containing a very dark, very frothy liquid.

'Well, now I'm back, maybe I could pop round sometime,' said Karl on the phone.

Why not? I thought, and then we could have a Karl party. Who knows, I might even have some other cousin Karls knocking about.

The Karl on the phone went on, 'Well look, I've got a new mobile number, do you want to jot it down?'

In a kind of trance I scribbled the number on the pad. And Karl on the phone sounded good fun; much more likeable than the other one, who was watching me with a curious, impatient look on his face. But which one of them was genuine? Because one of them had to be an impostor.

And why exactly was someone pretending to be Karl anyway?

I said goodbye to Karl Mark Two, while Karl Mark One asked who was on the phone.

I longed to say, 'Well, *you* actually,' but I had to play this very carefully. So I said vaguely, 'Oh, just a mate telling me his new mobile number.' Karl wasn't really listening anyway. Instead, he said firmly, 'Now, here's the tonic your parents want you to drink.' Then he beckoned me into the kitchen and thrust the glass at me.

Up to now the sheer weirdness of every-thing had stopped me being scared. But quite suddenly I was terrified. Here I was, in what could well be the greatest danger of my life. Time for me to act like a hero – and hide. But I couldn't even do that. Not with Karl right in front of me, while that potion continued to froth and bubble menacingly.

'Funny they never mentioned this brew to me,' I said.

'They've been very busy,' said Karl, 'but I know they're anxious for you to try this . . . and so am I.'

I was holding the glass now and Karl was watching me with such an intense, keen look. This worried me. And the fact that he almost certainly wasn't Cousin Karl worried me even more.

'Well, before I drink this lovely-looking brew,' I said, 'I'd like to propose a toast to us and our friendship. I can call you a friend, can't I?'

'Of course you can,' said Karl.

'Well, who'd have thought we'd be such great mates, especially as we haven't seen each other for such a long time, not since Cousin Charlie's wedding, in fact.' I said this so casually, but I've never waited more expectantly for an answer to a question.

Karl replied with just two words. 'That's right.'

But it was enough. For I haven't got a Cousin Charlie. It was at Cousin Fred's wedding we'd last met. The real Cousin Karl would definitely have known that. So that meant this impostor had wormed his way into my house because ... HE WAS A VAMPIRE.

The words just exploded into my head. There couldn't be any other explanation. It wasn't the headmaster. It wasn't Tallulah. It was KARL. And Karl had been waiting impatiently around here all these days for a top-up of my blood. And now that moment had clearly arrived.

I wanted to yell, scream and faint, all at once. And my head was spinning so much I nearly lost my balance. One thing saved me: I wasn't just very, very scared. I was absolutely furious as well.

How dare he strut about my house, bore me rigid and be a blood-sucking fiend! Well, I wasn't having it.

So, my heart thumping furiously, I said, 'Here's to us: mates to the end.' Then I gave the drink a massive jolt and threw it all over the floor. Not a drop of it was left.

'Ooops, clumsy me,' I cried.

'What did you do that for?' he demanded angrily.

'Ooh, a few reasons really,' I said, my anger still spurring me on. 'But the killer reason, I suppose, is that I've just been chatting to you on the phone.'

'What are you talking about?'

'Yeah, it was most odd. There was another person calling himself Cousin Karl—'

'An impostor,' he snapped, a new sharpness in his voice.

'No offence, but actually I think he's the real one and you . . . well, you're a . . .'

But even before I'd said the dreaded word, his eyes began turning a horrifyingly red colour.

'Don't move,' he cried.

Advice I firmly intended to disregard, but I reckoned without the force of those eyes, which just clamped themselves on to me. And I couldn't look away from his gaze. It seemed to overwhelm and take me over.

Then I felt my head start to rock slowly from side to side, just as if he was about to hypnotize me. I couldn't let that happen. I had to fight back. I could hear him breathing really loudly as he edged towards me.

'Not too close,' I muttered, 'because your strong breath is rotting all my nasal hairs.'

'Why have you always got to try and be funny?' he sighed. 'You've no idea how weary I get of your constant inane remarks all the time.' He sounded really aggrieved.

'I'm so sorry,' I said, desperately trying to stop my head from swaying about. 'But then you're a typical vampire – absolutely no sense of humour. You *are* a vampire, aren't you?'

'Oh, yes,' he hissed proudly, 'but living quietly and respectably until I sensed a very ripe half-vampire.'

Karl still spoke with that irritating super-confidence, but there was an odd calmness about him too, as if he knew he was in perfect control of this situation.

'So you've just been pretending to be Karl?'

He nodded. 'I've been tracking you. I heard your parents whispering outside about this Cousin Karl and his family and whether they could help. I spotted your mother posting a letter which I made sure they never received. I stole it off their mat.'

'You daredevil,' I said scornfully.

'And then I discovered this Karl and all his family were far away in America. I also found out he was exactly the same age as me. *And* he actually bore a very slight resemblance to me.'

'Poor guy,' I muttered.

'But could I pose as him? That was a risk, but your parents hadn't seen him for so long,

187

and in the end they were just very relieved that someone might be able to help their idiot son.'

I ignored this insult and asked, 'But why bother with all this pretending? Why not just lie in wait for me one dark and gloomy night?'

Karl actually shuddered. 'Vampires do have certain standards. Surely you know that.'

'Oh yeah,' I said, laughing cynically. 'You don't like taking blood from someone you haven't been introduced to. How incredibly polite you are, for a blood-sucking weirdo.'

'Vampires like to do things properly,' said Karl, 'and prefer to be invited into the homes of our blood donors first.'

'So you wangle yourself into my house on false pretences and then attack me in the woods.'

'I did nothing of the sort,' said Karl crisply. 'I merely called upon someone I knew and asked him to share some of his blood with me.'

I laughed derisively and noticed something else: my head wasn't rocking so fast. Perhaps if I kept him talking a bit longer I could break this spell he'd cast over me – and run for my life.

'I was very careful,' said Karl, 'not to take too much.'

'Well, you got your blood,' I said, 'so why are you still here?'

'I'm afraid your blood was so exquisite I could think of nothing else.' That intent look came into his face again. 'I must have more. But I was very worried that you might turn into a half-vampire before I got my second chance. And half-vampire blood tastes even worse than an ordinary human's. So I decided to return again and pretend to help.'

'But all the time you were trying to put me off from changing over,' I said. 'Well, you did a great job. I don't think I've ever met a more annoying person than you.'

'And I can return the compliment,' he replied with a faint smile. 'I knew how much you disliked me.'

'And that's putting it mildly.'

'So I made sure you saw as much of me as possible. It wasn't easy though. Your constant stream of stupid, inane comments . . .' He shook his head. 'So when your parents left me in charge I decided to strike. And, suitably refreshed after my rest, I'm ready to do full justice to your blood – NOW!' He suddenly shouted the last word, making me jump.

'I suppose that so-called tonic was to put me to sleep?'

'Yes, and it's such a shame you didn't take it. Then you could have donated your blood to me quite painlessly.'

'Painlessly!' I exclaimed. 'I'd have been ill for ages afterwards.'

'I'm sure you would have recovered . . . eventually,' he said. 'But now we're going to have to do this the hard way.'

No, I thought, we're not going to do this at all, because my head had stopped rocking completely.

So here was my moment to break free. Should I make for the front door? But Karl had locked that earlier, and had the key. Then I remembered I hadn't closed the window in the sitting room. I could slip out of there in a couple of seconds and then just leg it.

I had to do that.

Karl leaned even closer to me.

And then suddenly his fangs appeared. They were huge and jagged and looked painfully sharp.

'Those fangs,' I said, 'don't do anything for you. Ever thought of getting a brace?'

'Inane chatter, all the time,' he sighed. 'Now, don't move,' he said sharply, like a command.

But that's exactly what I did. 'Not today, thank you,' I said, and burst out of the kitchen door and towards the lounge.

Only I never reached it as—

Sorry, but I've got to stop here a second.

CHAPTER EIGHTEEN

10.15 p.m.

Now I'm back.

It's just the next bit is really painful for me, even now.

You see, I almost escaped from Karl. I'd whizzed out of that kitchen at great speed, and I'm sure I could have got to safety if something hadn't suddenly dropped down onto me in the hallway.

Then there was a swirl of dark wings. And the huge bat I'd seen before was back. Only this time the bat didn't just attack me. No, it writhed and flapped dementedly across my face and then flew straight into my hair. I desperately tried to swat it away.

But the bat just kept coming back.

This was just a little show of power on Karl's part really. The bat even made weird, high squeaks as it charged at me, as if it were having a marvellous time.

'Go away,' I yelled, hoping I sounded much braver than I felt, 'and fly back to a Dracula film.'

And then *splat*, I felt something hit my neck just as it had done that night in the woods. The bat had aimed its venom at me again. I could actually feel it seeping down my neck. I instantly staggered back.

In a few milliseconds I'll have passed out, I thought, and Karl will . . . But no, I couldn't let that happen. I mustn't give up. Got to do something . . .

Frantically I tried to wipe off the poison on my neck. And then . . . my mobile went off. Energy powered into me as I snatched it out of my pocket and saw the caller was Tallulah.

'Help!' I croaked.

'I just called to check you got—' began Tallulah. Then she stopped. '*What* did you just say?'

'End this conversation now or you'll be

very sorry.' Karl was back in his human form again and standing right beside me. He was looking at me with a kind of wild fury. But do you know what, he didn't really scare me; not then. He was going to feed off me anyway, I thought. So what more could he do to me?

I hissed. 'You were right . . . so right.'

Tallulah picked up on this immediately. 'The vampire . . . he's real, isn't he?'

'Yeah,' I croaked. There could be no disagreement on that point.

'He's not there with you now, is he?'

'Yes,' I croaked again before Karl tried to grab the phone from me. But incredibly I was too quick. I turned away from him and held the phone really tightly.

'Marcus!' Tallulah sounded both scared and very excited. 'Is it in your house now?'

'Oh yes.' Karl was circling right beside me again. 'But I know you'll find a window of opportunity . . .' That was my hint that the sitting-room window was still open. I didn't want to be too explicit or Karl would just immediately close it.

Tallulah started to ask me something else, but Karl suddenly yanked the phone from me and sent it spinning across the floor.

'Hey, if you have broken that you'll pay for a new one,' I cried.

'Who was that?' he demanded.

'Wrong number.'

'It was that girl. What were you saying to her?'

'You heard me,' I said.

He considered for a moment. 'Well, even if she does ring on the doorbell, so what?' Then he smacked his lips. I almost tasted his desperate impatience. He was so hungry for my blood now he couldn't think about anything else.

Karl half guided, half pushed me back to the kitchen. Then I sank slowly into a chair, my head hammering with deep tiredness.

Blearily I could see him hovering expectantly over me, expecting me to pass out any second. Somehow I had to push back this great tide of sleep flooding over me. I took some deep breaths.

'Why do you always have to make things difficult?' sighed Karl.

'Oh, I'm very sorry to inconvenience you.'

'Why drag this out?' he demanded. 'Just let sleep take you over.'

But I was choosy about who dined on my blood and Karl wasn't getting another drop if I could help it. I had to stay awake until Tallulah got here. I was sure she'd come round my house. But had she picked up the hint about the open window? Well, even if she just kept ringing on the doorbell that might distract Karl and give me the chance to escape. Oh, who was I kidding? I could barely walk now, let alone run to safety.

Still, I just had to stay awake, at least delay things. I started doing my deep breathing again, my breath coming now in hard gasps.

Karl glared down at me, a look of cold hatred in his eyes. 'I try and do things the civilized way, because that's my style. And I think vampires should be friendly with their donors – but you have left me with no other choice.'

'What do you mean?' I murmured.

'I can wait no longer. Now this will not be at all pleasant for you. And the side effects of a double dose can last a long time. But as I said, you've left me no other choice. And very regretfully, I must change form again.'

So a second poison dart was beaming its way to me. And there was nothing I could do about it this time.

But then, in a very short space of time, three incredible things happened.

The first was Tallulah bursting into the kitchen. 'Marcus!' she yelled. 'Here I am.'

I peered up at her, my heart hammering with relief. She was wearing a thick coat and a very determined expression on her face. Shock waves ripped through the whole room. Karl's body went completely still. He looked hugely confused as well. 'How did she—?' he began.

'Ah, wouldn't you like to know?' I gasped. Tallulah crouched down beside me. 'You got here just in the nick of time,' I said. 'And by the way, meet a genuine, fang-carrying foul-smelling vampire.'

'I knew vampires existed,' cried Tallulah jubilantly. 'I just *knew* it. But I've met you before .. you're the cousin.'

'Second cousin,' I corrected. 'Only he was just pretending to be him. And he's such a big fan of my blood that he's back for a second helping. He's also very cross that I'm not asleep yet.'

'Shut up,' said Karl. He raised his nose up, as if sniffing the air. But I guessed he was thinking hard. He glared at Tallulah. 'I *knew* you were trouble when you came round before,' he hissed.

'I have always wanted to meet a vampire,' said Tallulah, standing up and staring at Karl.

'Well, you can exchange email addresses later,' I said.

'But I can't let you hurt my friend,' she went on.

I liked the way Tallulah said 'friend' so warmly. And she was about to say something else when she stopped. Instead, her whole face froze with horror.

And then I caught sight of Karl and realized why.

His face was truly the most terrifying I'd ever seen. His deep-red eyes now seemed to have sunk right into the back of his head. And they had no expression in them at all. In fact, his whole face had just closed up.

It was as if the human disguise Karl wore

198

had checked out, leaving only a vampire behind: a vampire grown savage with rage and hunger. Now he looked like a very dangerous animal who was about to attack a human, something vampires only did in extreme circumstance. But I knew this was one of them.

He didn't want Tallulah's blood at all, but he would take it as an act of revenge for her getting in his way and stopping him drinking my blood.

As Karl advanced towards Tallulah, she didn't move. She couldn't. He'd hypnotized her with his dead eyes, exactly as he had done with me.

And I was just so mad with myself. Why did I tell Tallulah to come here? What could she possibly do against a fully-fledged vampire? And did I really think Karl was going to let Tallulah and me walk out of here together? Well, yes, I did actually. I'd thought, as soon as he saw Tallulah, that he'd realize the game was up and just go – but instead . . .

Instead, Tallulah was now in the greatest danger of her whole life.

Karl advanced towards Tallulah's pale throat. His mouth was open. His fangs gleamed and shone.

'Let her go, Karl,' I cried. 'You can have my blood – gallons of it – and mine's the kind you specially like.'

'Oh yes, I shall have your blood too,' murmured Karl. 'But she has annoyed me so much that in this instance I shall drink some vile, human blood first.'

'You're just sick,' I cried.

'This is no time to start flattering me,' he purred, sounding even more nauseatingly smug than usual.

I staggered to my feet. But Karl wasn't bothered. In fact, he even turned his back on me. He knew I couldn't really do anything against him and his super powers.

Anger and rage I'd never felt before leaped into the pit of my stomach. It rose up through my chest and into my throat, where it burst with such fury I really thought I was going to have a choking fit.

But instead, that's when the second incredible thing happened.

CHAPTER NINETEEN

Monday 22 October
10.18 p.m.

I let out a howl.

The loudest, wildest, longest, deepest, most spine-shivering, most blood-curdling howl you've ever heard. I tell you it just blasted into that room with such force that Karl leaped back from Tallulah as if I'd just landed one almighty punch on him.

And then I did exactly that. Suddenly and totally amazingly, I let out a second roar (nearly as impressive as my first one), charged forward, grabbed Karl and then hurled a punch at his chest, knocking all the wind out of him, immediately followed by a second punch, which sent him flying across the room.

Tallulah was gazing at me while clutching her neck. 'I really thought he was going to . . . and I couldn't move. It was so . . .' Then she saw Karl sprawled out on the floor by the kitchen table. 'Did someone else just come in here and do that?'

I shook my head. 'No. All my own work.'

'And that roar you let out – it made my ears pop. You're amazing. I can't believe it.'

Actually I was having trouble believing it too. I felt dead strange as well, quite unlike myself. It was as if a thunderstorm had just erupted right inside my head, shaking me up so much that I'd become someone entirely different.

But Karl started leaning slowly forward. 'You won't hit me again,' he snarled.

'Yes, I will,' I said, standing over him with my fists bunched together.

It was then Tallulah rushed forward and said, 'Don't worry, Marcus, I've come armed. Look!'

She flung off her coat. 'The hardware shop

was out of stakes,' she said cheerfully, 'so I bought these instead at the grocery shop.' And then came the third incredible event as Tallulah brought out tons and tons of garlic. 'Emptied the place,' she said proudly. 'There's not a strong-smelling garlic clove left in the shop.' And she started firing these garlic cloves at Karl.

Karl pitched to the ground again and let out a shriek of horror as the garlic cloves rained down on him. 'Stop it,' he urged in a low, ragged voice, and put his hands up to his face to protect him from any more. But Tallulah seemed to have an inexhaustible supply of garlic.

'Marcus, look at his face,' she shouted suddenly.

Karl's eyes had practically vanished and his skin looked all crumpled and ancient. He was shrivelling away in front us.

'Wow, he's turning into the oldest man in the world. Isn't this fantastic?' cried Tallulah.

'Oh yes,' I agreed. I'd have said it a bit more enthusiastically if the garlic smell wasn't making me feel a bit nauseous too. 'I'll just sit down here for a second,' I said, trying to move as far away from the ghastly smell as I could.

And then suddenly something else came splashing onto the floor: sick – vampire-style. Bright green with what looked like tiny red spots inside it.

'Oh, this is tremendous,' cried Tallulah, studying it. 'Come and look, Marcus.'

'You're all right,' I said, fearing if I saw it I'd soon be adding to it.

'Now, listen to me,' said Tallulah to a now very aged and seedy-looking Karl. 'I've also got garlic powder in my coat. And I'm willing to use it as well if you don't start answering a few questions, like: Why have you come here? Come on, speak!'

Karl made a noise like a cross between a howl and a very loud belch and then vanished.

'He's gone,' shouted Tallulah, deeply disappointed.

'No, he hasn't,' I said. 'He's a marvellous quick-change vampire. He'll be a bat again now – yeah, look, there he is!'

And there was the bat, not moving so confidently this time though. It swayed, rather than swirled around the room. Then all at once it seemed to go very still as it hovered in the darkest corner of the room.

'Got you,' cried Tallulah, lunging at it. But instead it disappeared again. Only this time it just seemed to melt away into the darkness. Or maybe the dark swallowed it up. Anyway, it had vanished – gone.

'He didn't answer any of my questions,' said Tallulah sadly.

I immediately started packing up the garlic. 'All right if I bung this outside for now?' I said. 'It just reminds me of him.'

'OK,' said Tallulah. 'And keep it – I don't want it.' I knew for certain we didn't want it either. I hurled it onto the back patio, nearly throwing up as well. How anyone could ever buy garlic, I don't know. The smell is truly appalling.

'Do you think he'll come back for his clothes and stuff?' asked Tallulah.

'I doubt it,' I said.

'So do I,' she said. 'Vampires are almost always quite rich. So he'll just buy a load of new clothes.' Then she let out a cry of disappointment. 'His vomit has disappeared.'

'Oh, what a cruel blow. What were you planning to do with that?'

'Study it,' said Tallulah. 'Put it under a microscope.'

'Yuck,' I said.

'But don't you see, we've no proof now that a vampire really was here. Apart from us, of course,' she sighed. 'I'd love to have found out more about him.'

'There wasn't really time for a nice cosy chat – he was too busy trying to drink up my blood . . . and yours.'

'What a night,' she sighed appreciatively.

'If you hadn't come round tonight I certainly wouldn't be alive. Great you got my hint about the window.'

'Wasn't difficult,' she said.

'And the garlic was an inspired idea.'

'For me, it was just obvious. But then, as I told you, I'm an expert on vampires. And to think you had one living all that time in your house.'

'Yeah, he had us all fooled. You see, we hadn't seen the real Cousin Karl for years. Then the real one rang up tonight. That was a very weird moment, I can tell you. The fake one said he'd never attack a stranger.'

'That's right, they like to be introduced to you first,' said Tallulah. She looked at me. 'What I don't get is why the vampire chose you.'

I hesitated for a second, and then said quietly, 'Well, I don't like to boast, but I've got amazing blood—'

'No, be serious,' interrupted Tallulah. 'That vampire was just wasted on you. And it could come back.'

'I didn't like the way you smiled when you said that,' I said.

'No, you're still in danger. You'll definitely need a bodyguard; someone who knows all about vampires.'

'Are you volunteering for the job?' I asked.

'Of course I am.' Tallulah grinned. 'Have you got a spare room?'

'We've got the attic.'

'Perfect. I'll live there. And you needn't pay me. My parents will pay you to get shot of me.'

'If your parents had seen you tonight they'd have been well impressed,' I said. 'Just as I am.'

Tallulah actually beamed at me then. In fact, the whole room seemed soaked in happiness.

And then . . . and then my parents came back.

CHAPTER TWENTY

11.30 p.m.

'Don't panic,' called out Tallulah, 'but your son's just been attacked by a vampire. Now, don't worry, I dealt with the situation and he's absolutely fine.'

'It's true,' I added. 'Karl was, in fact, not my cousin – but a vampire.'

My mum and dad gaped at Tallulah and me in total confusion. We went into the sitting room, and by the time Tallulah and I had finished telling them about Karl's attack, both my parents had aged about ten years. They looked terrible. They whispered to me how they hadn't been able to find the specialist Karl had recommended, but just thought they'd got the address down wrong.

'How could we have left him in charge?' cried Mum.

'We should have asked him for proof of identity or something,' said Dad.

'Oh, Dad, who'd want to live in a world where people did things like that?' I said. 'He knew all about the letter we'd sent and he was the same age as the real Karl – of course you believed him.'

'Vampires are very clever,' put in Tallulah. 'I'm an expert on them.' Then she added kindly, 'I don't suppose you even thought they existed up to now, did you?'

'No,' murmured Dad, and then he got up. 'You two have had a nasty shock; you both deserve a hot drink now.'

'Oh, that's all right,' began Tallulah.

'No, I insist,' said Dad. He marched off to the kitchen, while Mum continued asking about tonight, but she seemed distracted. I guessed she was just really shocked by what had happened. Then Dad returned. 'Hot chocolate, perfect at a moment like this.'

He seemed to perk up now as he chatted away to Tallulah and me. 'I want to thank you, Tallulah,' he said, 'for all you've done tonight. We will always be very grateful to you.'

'And you do believe it was a vampire?' asked Tallulah.

'Oh, yes,' said Dad, 'we're certain of that.'

'And will you tell other people?' went on Tallulah.

'Why not?' said Dad smoothly and without a moment's hesitation – which stunned me.

And then something happened which shocked me much more.

Tallulah suddenly gave a large yawn. 'Oh, sorry,' she cried, and then gave an even larger yawn and her head slumped forward.

I sprang to my feet. 'Was there something in that drink?'

'It's all right,' said Dad.

'No it's not all right,' I said. 'You can't go around drugging my friends.'

'It's very mild,' said Mum. She and Dad were leaning over Tallulah now. 'And we only use it in emergencies.'

'And this *is* an emergency,' said Dad. Then he muttered to Mum, 'How long did the manual say to wait?'

'Five minutes is their recommended time,' said Mum.

'And then what?' I exclaimed.

'First,' said Dad, 'you must tell us exactly what Tallulah knows.'

'Why?' I asked.

'Oh come on, Ved,' said Mum, 'you must see that we can't allow Tallulah to know vampires exist. She will talk about today – and very loudly. And then people will descend on us, wanting to know all the details, such as why you were picked out. Suddenly we'd be the focus of everybody's attention. Half-vampires can't live like that.'

'Too much to hide, you mean,' I said bitterly. I hated seeing poor Tallulah lying there, drugged. It wasn't right, after all she'd done to save me tonight.

'You've got to help us,' said Mum, 'and there isn't much time.'

'But first of all,' I replied, 'you've got to tell me what you're going to do to her.'

They did.

After which I explained how Tallulah had seen the mark of the vampire bite on my neck that night in the woods, and again when she visited me here. I told them too how I'd met her earlier tonight (both my parents shook their heads gravely and Mum muttered, 'To go out when you're "in season". How foolish is that?').

Then Dad said, 'I'm now going to talk to Tallulah. But it's very important that the only voice she hears is mine.'

'The manual was very firm about that,' cut in Mum. 'Said it could confuse her gravely . . . so not a word, Ved.'

'All right,' I muttered.

Dad then leaned next to Tallulah and said in a slow, calm voice, 'Good evening, Tallulah, can you hear me?'

'Yes,' she said.

'Please repeat everything I say.'

'Please repeat everything I say,' said Tallulah.

'I never saw the mark of the vampire on V—' Dad nearly said 'Ved', but just in time said, 'Marcus's neck.'

'I never saw the mark of the vampire on V— Marcus's neck.'

Dad repeated this instruction one more time just to make sure it was completely clear.

Next he said, 'And I never saw a vampire here tonight.'

'And I never saw a vampire here tonight,' repeated Tallulah.

This went on for quite a bit longer. And in the end I had to walk away. I knew what my parents meant about keeping the identity of vampires and half-vampires secret. I could see why they had to hypnotize Tallulah. But I still hated watching it, and especially the way Tallulah recited everything in that drab, lifeless voice, nothing like her own.

Then Dad clapped his hands and Tallulah woke up. She looked around in some surprise.

'It was so good of you,' said Mum, 'to come round to see how Marcus is.'

'And to let us thank you personally,' said Dad, shaking hands with her, 'for finding Marcus when he fell over in the woods.'

'That's all right,' said Tallulah, sounding like someone just waking up in the morning. 'But I'd better go now.'

'I'll see you out,' I said. At the door I asked, 'So how are you?'

'Absolutely fine – why are you suddenly asking me that?'

'Oh, I always ask people that after they've spent time with my parents. So where are you off to now?'

'Home,' she said wearily.

'And do you remember where that is?'

She looked at me. 'What are you talking about? Trying to be funny as usual, I suppose.' And with that she left.

I told my dad I was going to trail her just to check she ended up returning to the right house. But he said I mustn't, under any circumstances, go out, as I was still very weak. So he followed her instead. And she did find her way home without any problems at all.

'I told you,' said Mum, 'she won't suffer any ill effects.'

Only she won't remember offering to be my bodyguard. And that's a massive shame, blog. I'd loved to have seen her doing that.

Tuesday 23 October
9.00 a.m.

Slept in quite late this morning.

I was finally woken by a funny sort of itching on my lip. I leaped out of bed.

And there it was: one yellow fang. I blinked at it in total amazement and joy. 'Class,' I murmured. Then I tore downstairs. Dad and Mum were both in the kitchen.

'Fangs away,' I said.

CHAPTER TWENTY-ONE

9.45 a.m.

If you ever want to stop your parents gassing on and on, here's a tip for you – grow a fang. It really shuts them up.

They both just stared and stared at me, and then Dad blew his nose twice, while Mum gulped and cried and got the hiccups.

'Be honest now,' I said. 'You never thought this moment would happen, did you? Well, don't worry, because I didn't either.'

And still my parents couldn't utter a single word. It was embarrassing and shocking and brilliant, all at once.

The doctor's just given me a check-up. Only Mum and Dad left us alone this time.

10.50 a.m.

'Well, this is a day of rejoicing in the Howlett household,' Dr Jasper said. 'The caterpillar has finally broken out of its chrysalis.' He peered at my fang through his magnifying glass. 'That looks very healthy indeed.'

'So will it grow any more?' I asked.

'Unlikely,' said the doctor. 'If it feels itchy, I've left some ointment – but do not scratch it. Let the fang do its good work. It'll slip off in three days. And you must stay indoors for at least another week.' He leaned forward. 'Being different is never easy.'

'Oh, when you're a genius like me you get used to it,' I said. Then I added breezily, 'Who wants to be normal anyway?'

He looked at me. 'Well, it's my belief there's no such thing as a normal person. I've certainly never met one. We're all unusual and different in some way, thank goodness.'

'Last night, Doc, I got really mad and let out a howl Count Dracula would have envied. Is that why I crossed over?'

'Let's say the wall you'd put up around yourself came crashing down last night and woke you up,' he said. 'You suddenly realized you had all this untapped power and strength. Now magic really does run in your blood. Welcome to the world of half-vampires.'

We solemnly shook hands.

'There are some little problems with being a half-vampire,' he said, 'but take my advice and never look on it as a burden. Instead, befriend that part of yourself and you will see you have also been given a great gift.'

Wednesday 24 October
11.50 a.m.

Mum is getting rid of all Karl's clothes and belongings. I ask if I can keep his magnificent cape. 'You want another one?' cries Mum.

'Yeah, I've always wanted to be a two-cape half-vampire.'

Mum smiles. 'Oh, why not?'

But I'm not intending to keep it for myself.

3.00 p.m.

My nan has rung up from France. 'I always knew you had it in you.'

'You were the only one then,' I replied.

Cousin Karl (the real one) has also called and said we must get together properly soon. And he congratulated me on a big moment in my life.

I suddenly thought again of Tallulah. I owed her so much. And yet she wouldn't remember one second of how she'd saved me from Karl.

Friday 26 October
2.50 a.m.

I was woken up by Dad waving a torch in my face. 'Yes, yes,' he said excitedly to my mum. 'There it is.'

'Don't mind me,' I said. 'Just relax and enjoy yourselves.'

'Sorry, dear, but we just wanted to keep your fang safe,' said Mum.

It had fallen out of my mouth and was now nestling on my pillow. Dad picked it up as if it were a piece of gold. Then Mum put it carefully into a little gold box. It had my name on the outside and the date. Next they both produced gold boxes containing their yellow fangs. Actually, once you've seen one yellow fang you've seen them all. But still, it was good to be part of the fang gang.

And I'm not messing about. It really was. I mean, when I first heard about this half-vampire lark, it was the grisliest news I'd ever had. I was seriously creeped out. But now I've had the chance to get used to it, I . . . I'm going to try and make the best of it all.

Anyway, then Dad handed me an envelope. 'Hey, I haven't got another name, have I?'

'Look inside,' said Dad.

Inside was fifty pounds.

'Hey, that's better than being called Ved,' I said. 'By the way, can I just say that I still hate that name, and I'd much rather be called Marcus.'

But my parents looked away and carried on speaking as though I hadn't said a word. That's one of their little tricks. When I say something they don't like, they just ignore me. So I suppose, disappointingly, some things haven't changed at all.

CHAPTER TWENTY-TWO

**Wednesday 31 October, Halloween
10.15 p.m.**

For the first time in several centuries I'm allowed out of the house. I'm back at school tomorrow, and tonight I was at the Monsters in School meeting, to have another go at telling my gory tale.

We all arrived in our masks, of course. I'd borrowed Joel's vampire one again. But Tallulah was in a dead funny mood, especially at the start of the meeting when Joel asked, 'After this, will we be able to go off and do trick or treat?'

Tallulah jumped to her feet and cried, 'Trick or treat? That's for four-year-olds who like dressing up as pumpkins to get chocolate buttons.'

'And me,' said Joel bravely.

'Joel, I'd rather have someone stick pins in my eyes in the most agonizing way possible than go out and play trick or treat. But you go if you want.'

'No, I'll just sit here and die quietly,' said Joel.

'Much better,' she snapped.

Next came the big moment, only this time I'd really worked on my story (with a great deal of help from Joel) and I stormed it – I think.

Everyone liked it, apart from Tallulah. I mean, she didn't say anything bad about it, but she didn't say she liked it either. I even wondered if she'd really listened to it as she was so vague about the whole thing. She did ask if I would stay behind at the end.

'You're in,' said Joel confidently.

But I wasn't so sure.

After everyone else had gone Tallulah said to me, 'Well, you have passed your audition and are now a member of Monsters in School.'

But she didn't say it very excitedly. Indeed, I still felt her mind was elsewhere. So I acted enthusiastically enough for both of us.

'Well, that's great news . . . in fact, the greatest news I've had for a long time. Thank you.' Then I added, 'By the way, I brought you a little gift. I didn't want to offer it to you before in case you thought it was a bribe.' Then I dug in my bag and brought out a cape. The cape Karl had left behind.

'For me?' she said, astonished.

'Yeah, I wanted to thank you for finding me that night in the woods' (she at least still remembered that) 'and getting help, because if you hadn't, well, I might have been kidnapped by robins or mugged by a sparrow. So, thanks.'

'This cape is brilliant,' she said, examining it.

'Well, it's not new,' I said. 'It belonged to . . . someone I knew who doesn't want it any more. So there you are.'

'Don't you want it yourself?' she asked.

'No, it's yours.'

'But this is incredible.' She sat down on her chair again.

'Glad you like it.'

'No, it's not just that.' She took off her head, I mean her mask. And I thought it was only polite for me to remove my vampire mask too.

'If I tell you something,' she said, 'you won't laugh, will you?'

'OK,' I said.

'Do you promise?'

'Yeah,' I grinned. 'Come on, spill.'

She still hesitated.

'Look, I promise I won't laugh. Guide's honour.'

A flicker of a smile crossed her face. 'You're such an idiot. That's why it doesn't make any sense.'

'Just tell me.'

Then she said quietly, 'Every night lately I've had dreams about vampires . . . and you.'

A little shiver ran through me. 'Tell me more.'

'Well, in one dream when I found you in the woods, you had the mark of a vampire on your neck. And then later when I visited you at your house, I saw the mark again.'

'You know what that means?' I said.

'No.'

'You're dreaming about the two things you like best in the world: vampires and me.'

She immediately shook her head. 'I knew you'd be silly.'

'Sorry.'

'And then last night . . .'

'You had another dream?' I prompted.

'Yes.'

'So what happened this time?'

Tallulah frowned. 'There was a mad vampire in your house. It was going to attack you – and you stopped it by letting out this incredibly scary howl. I ask you, how likely is that? I've heard you howl. And even when you try it's not good. In fact, it's pathetic.'

I agreed and then – well, I just couldn't resist it and I let out a howl that was at least as eerie as the one the night I attacked Karl.

Tallulah just gaped and gaped at me. She was numb with shock. Finally she stuttered, 'You've been practising.'

'And do you detect any improvement?'

'That was, without doubt, the best howl I have ever heard. And from you of all people.'

'I know.'

'It's just like the one in my dream too. How weird is that?'

'Very,' I agreed.

A smile slowly crossed her face: a big, really happy smile. 'Every day my life is just so dull and normal I have to force it to be even a little bit interesting by thinking about monsters. But somehow I just know it's about to be very very interesting all by itself.' Then Tallulah stretched out her hand. 'I'm really pleased you're in Monsters in School.'

'So am I,' I cried, shaking her hand. 'And keep dreaming about me, won't you?'

11.50 p.m.

I don't suppose you've ever been for a night-time flit, have you? Well, I hadn't until tonight.

Let me show off a bit and tell you what happens. First of all, you open a downstairs window. Then you start walking about in the kitchen or somewhere else downstairs on tiptoe. Yes, you feel a bit stupid (and probably look even more stupid) but all at once you find you're not touching the ground at all. No, you're floating in the air. Then you relax and before you know it, you've whooshed up into the air and have changed shape into a bat.

I didn't flap very far tonight. But still it was incredible to be flying about as a bat, even for five minutes. After we got back my parents handed me an envelope.

'Not another one,' I said. 'What's in this one?'

'Open it and see,' said Dad.

There was a piece of paper with just one word on it: MARCUS.

'So what's all this about?' I asked.

'We believe you didn't like your half-vampire name,' said Dad.

'Hated it. I wouldn't call a caterpillar Ved.'

'So although it's not normal practice, we applied to have your true vampire name changed back,' said Mum.

'And today we found out we had been successful,' said Dad.

'So now I'm Marcus again. Well, thanks a zillion – I didn't think you were even listening to me moaning on and on.'

'A new half-vampire name calls for a toast,'

said Dad, 'especially at Halloween.'

And then he cracked open this little bottle of blood which he'd kept chilled for a special occasion like this.

Got to tell you, that blood trickled down my throat so easily and tasted even better than it had before: so velvety and creamy, like milk chocolate, but with just a hint of raspberries too.

Well, I thought, here I am downing blood with my parents. I really have joined the crazies. But I didn't mind; in fact I was even a bit proud at that moment to be a half-vampire.

Then Dad made another toast: 'To our wonderful son.'

'Hey, stop it, I'm blushing already,' I said.

'And to his very successful completion of Phase One . . .'

Right then I stopped toasting myself. 'Phase One . . .' I echoed. 'You're not telling me there's a Phase Two, are you?'

Mum and Dad just laughed. 'That's for another day,' said Mum, staring deeply into her glass of blood.

There is a Phase Two, isn't there? I can feel it in my fangs. And my top-secret blogging will have to go on.

But Hell's teeth, what's going to happen to me now, blog?

TRY SOME MORE OF PETE JOHNSON'S WONDERFUL BOOKS ...

'I sensed hot breath on my neck. It was right behind me. It'll get me; I must run faster ... faster ...'

THE GHOST DOG
by Pete Johnson

Only mad scientists in stories can create monsters, can't they? Not ten-year-old boys like Daniel. Well, not until the night of his spooky party when he and his friends make up a ghost story about a terrifying dog ...

It's a story made up to frighten Aaron – tough, big-headed Aaron. But to Dan's horror, what begins as a story turns into a nightmare. Each night the ghost dog – a bloodthirsty, howling monster – haunts his dreams, and Dan suspects that what he conjured up with his imagination has somehow become ... real!

A spooky tale filled with chills and thrills, from top children's author Pete Johnson.

ISBN: 978 0 440 86341 0

Two spine-tingling tales from an award-winning author

PHANTOM FEAR
by Pete Johnson

The Phantom Thief

A mysterious boy appears as if from nowhere in the school detention room. A warning message is scratched on the blackboard by a phantom hand. Is Alfie in danger . . . ?

My Friend's a Werewolf

There's something odd about Kelly's new friend Simon – he wears gloves all the time and howls at night. But werewolves only exist in stories . . . don't they?

'A howling good read'
Young Telegraph

'Prepare to be thoroughly spooked'
Daily Mail

ISBN: 978 0 440 86690 9

They think I'M a big problem. Wrong. THEY are!

HOW TO TRAIN YOUR PARENTS
by Pete Johnson

Louis can't handle it any more. His new school is
Swotsville and his mum and dad have fallen into
some very bad ways. All they seem to care about now
is how well he's doing at school (answer: not well)
and what after-school clubs he wants to join (answer:
none!). They're no longer interested in his jokes (his
dream is to be a comedian) and have even nicked the
telly out of his bedroom!

What's going on? And can new friend Maddy help? For
Maddy tells him her parents used to behave equally
badly until she trained them. All parents have to be
trained - and she knows a foolproof way . . .

ISBN: 978 0 440 86439 4

PAY UP ON MONDAY OR ELSE . . .

TRAITOR
by Pete Johnson

What would you do if a gang of bullies decided to
waylay you on your way home from school,
demanding money? Would you pay up?

That's what Tom, Mia and Oliver do – at first.
Ashamed of being victims, united in their fear of the
gang, they feel powerless to do anything else. But as
the pressure builds more and more, a terrible suspicion
begins to surface: could one of the three friends be
helping the bullies? And if so, just who is . . . the
traitor?

ISBN: 978 0 440 86438 7